EXPERT ASSISTANCE

by

Robert Collins

Robert Collins

ISBN (10): 1456510088
ISBN (13): 978-1456510084

Cover by M. Mrakota Orsman (www.mirthquake.net)

Published in the United States of America
January 2011

First published by Asylett Press
January 2007

One
Hired!

Questor Corporation's space station Q-12 strongly resembled a yes-man. It was small as corporate stations went, with only six dual-ship docking ports connected by the slenderest of transit tubes. In the middle of the six spindly spokes was a fragile cylinder of low-cost composites. Q-12 was built by overworked accountants, cheap contractors, and economized constructor-bots. It screamed of dealmaking and pliant praise.

The "Skuld" was the latest starship to dock at Q-12. It was wildly out of place next to the station. Although much smaller than the station, it was dark, sleek, and tough. If Q-12 was built by accountants, Skuld was built by military officers in the field.

The starship was owned by one Jake Bonner. He was not a military man, but a working spacer. He was too smart to be recruited, and too in love with space to stay grounded. He had lucked across Skuld on his travels. He had hoped that its power would bring him profit.

He had not yet been so lucky.

As his ship docked with Q-12, Bonner walked onto the ship's bridge. It wasn't an accurate term, but it was the best he could come up with. The "bridge" was divided in two. One part was a conversation pit with a large video screen, a couch opposite that, and comfortable chairs surrounding them. Up a half-dozen steps was wide desk with two seats, lighted panels, complex displays, and sophisticated read-outs. Bonner plopped down in one of the seats and waited for the controlling computer to update him.

"The station is acknowledging," it reported a moment later. Its voice was clipped, precise, and a shade on the stuffy side.

"Patch us in, Odin." It was an obvious name for the computer; the ship's name was the Norse word for "future." "This is Jake Bonner, owner and operator of the free starship Skuld, requesting permission to dock, Q-12."

"Mr. Bonner, this is Station Q-12," a polite female voice answered. "Your identity is confirmed. Please stand by to be escorted in."

"Escorted? Why?"

"Our financial records show a debt of 8,467 cred-units owed, by you, to this station. You are hereby ordered not to leave this station until the debt is paid back in full. If your debts are not paid within seventy-two Earth-standard hours, your ship will be impounded.

"Thank you for visiting Q-112." The voice was actually earnest about the concluding sentiment.

Jake held off screaming at the station voice. He screamed at the computer instead. "Odin, why didn't you tell me I owed them 8,000 creds?"

"Because it is not my duty to watch over you. Or so you have repeatedly told me."

"Well, don't just idle, do something!"

"Your debt to the Questor chain has been logged into the main financial computer already. There is nothing legal that I can do."

"So do something illegal!"

"I refuse to engage in illegal operations just to prevent you from paying your obligations."

"Now, wait a minute here! Who owns who, anyway?"

"I suggest you cease this emotional display. Allow me to transfer the funds from your savings with Enterprise Banking, Insurance, and Salvage to the Questor Corporation."

"Oh, alright. How much is in there, anyway?"

"Eight hundred cred-units."

"All I have is a lousy eight hundred?"

"Not anymore. Your account is now drained."

"I thought there was 12,000 in there."

"There was. Seven days ago, your debts to Blake Stations, Incorporated, were paid off. By court order."

"One of these days I'm going to violently reformat your hard drives."

"I shall ignore that remark. I am making it known throughout the station that you are willing to take on employment on a cash-up-front basis."

Bonner held back a groan. He knew from long experience the quality of employment offered by those with ready credits. If the job wasn't illegal or immoral, it would be boring and simple. The choices would almost always be between bad and worse. And there he was, stuck making those choices again.

"This is going to be fun," he said morosely.

"Either this, or put me up for sale." Odin's tone left no doubt about his preference. "One moment, Jake. I have located a request that is enigmatic, to say the least. Shall I initiate contact?"

"I suppose. Don't bother with the main screen. I don't want to get up."

"Very well. Jake, please meet Daniel and Clarissa Rosen."

An instant later an man and a woman appeared on the upper-deck console screen. They were dressed alike in drab work coveralls. The man had dark hair, the woman dirty brown. Both seemed to be in their late twenties.

The man spoke first. "Mr. Bonner? Pleased to meet you. We're from the colony planet Antioch Two. Are you familiar with it?"

"No. Odin?"

"Antioch Two is a mining colony, owned by one Sordius Maxis. It's population is Class Six, and therefore not a part of the Interstellar Governing Convention. It has been operational for 107 years, and has shown a profit for the last 73."

"And do you know how that's possible, Mr. Bonner?" Clarissa asked hotly. "Maxis keeps us poorly fed and clothed, and claims the air is our pay!"

Jake heaved a mighty sigh. He wanted to shout out, "Are there no new pleas in this galaxy? Am I the only human who knows our history?" He had traveled far and wide through human space, so he had heard of oppressed worlds. His parents had given him an appreciation of the history of the human race, so he knew about rebellions, their causes, and their outcomes. So when Clarissa Rosen said what she did, Jake had no doubt what they were going to ask him to do.

It was, however, more than a little frustrating to know where the Rosens were heading. It meant that their job offer carried with it a rather predictable set of actions he would have to take: organization; subversion; then direct action against the regime. If what Clarissa said was true, each of these would be easy tasks to accomplish. There would be no real challenge to the job, just another go-through of the motions that have been carried on since time immemorial.

No, he reminded himself, *there would be one challenge: getting paid*. Rebels as a rule didn't have much on hand to compensate hired help. Getting into power might allow them to reward his work, but the odds were that the Rosens were from some podunk colony with an annual income only slightly higher that his present debt load. The compensation was fairly unlikely to equal the amount of work he'd have to put out to help them succeed.

He decided to let the couple down easy. But before doing that, Jake made certain that his hunch was correct. He said to them, "Let me guess. You want me to help you oust this Maxis, so you can replace him with a government that will respect the workers. Am I right?"

The couple's eyes went wide. "How did you know?"

"I have been around the galaxy a few times. Look, a hired gun isn't going to make a bit of difference."

"Mr. Bonner," Daniel said, "we are prepared to reward your assistance with five percent of our mines' profits, each year, for life."

"That's very kind of you,..."

Odin spoke up in a firm, soft tone. "Jake, if you were to receive five percent, you would earn 75,000 cred-units per year. Minimum. Assuming no crashes in the mineral markets, of course."

Jake needed a few seconds to comprehend the figure. "Seventy ...five... thousand...?" he stammered. "What do you people mine, diamonds?"

"Gold, actually."

"Antioch Two has the second largest gold veins in human space," Odin supplied calmly, "along with the fourth largest silver deposits, third richest copper deposits, and so on. Antioch Two appears to be an untapped source of vast wealth in precious minerals."

It took a moment, but Jake snapped out of his shock. When he did he realized that the couple had been surprised that he knew what they were going to ask before they asked it. *If they didn't know*, he reasoned, *they probably don't know how to go about waging a revolution. It will mean lots of work, but their offer will more than compensate for that.*

I'll be set for life, and I won't have to take boring jobs like this one anymore.

Pressing his shirt with his hands, Jake sat up straight. "Well, then, I suppose we should... no, we must strive to ensure that colonists on independent worlds are not denied their basic rights. I would be happy to do my part."

"We're glad you feel that way, Mr. Bonner," Clarissa said, seemingly oblivious to Jake's mood change. "We're prepared to advance you fifteen hundred creds."

"Fifteen-hundred? That won't get me to Antioch Two anytime soon. Can't you up that a little?"

"We can barely afford that, Mr. Bonner."

Jake grimaced. His opportunity for the easy life, his chance to stop wandering, his hopes for attracting a young and beautiful love slave, all threatened to sprout jump drives and zip away. He gritted his teeth. "I hate to say this, but..."

"I have uncovered a possible source of immediate income," Odin announced. "You may accept this assignment, if you wish."

"Thank you. I accept. Log your advance, and the other offer, and I'll get back to you as soon as possible. Skuld, out."

Jake let out a maniacal laugh. "I'm gonna be rich! Filthy rich! Odin, if you were a woman, I would marry you."

"I am pleased you have such a deep respect for my ability and talents."

"Oh, don't be so stuffy. Admit it, Odin. You wouldn't have guided me to this offer if you didn't like the idea of me becoming wealthy."

"Well, I admit that a more reliable source of income would allow for certain advances to my software and hardware."

"That's the spirit! Now, what's this other source of income?"

"The individual is on his way. One moment. The gentleman, Sidney Kraft, is in the airlock, and requests permission to board the ship."

"Let him in."

The man entered the bridge through the entranceway opposite the control area. Sidney Kraft might have been in his late thirties, but it was more likely that he was faking it. His hair was too neatly in place, his skin too tanned and smooth, and his shape too sculpted. His clothes reminded Jake of a pink Christmas tree.

"You Jake Bunter?" Sid asked. His voice was way too smooth.

"Bonner. Jake Bonner."

Oh, yeah, Bonner." Sid approached, took Jake's hand and shook it vigorously. "I'm Sid Kraft, of Kraft, Kropf, Kretz, and Bartholomew."

"What do you do? Why are you hiring?"

Kraft appeared mildly surprised. "I'm an agent, Mr. Burner."

"That's Bonner. What kind of agent?"

"Aw, come on! You gotta know about us. We're the top entertainment artist representation firm in the galaxy. We've got dozens of stars, from video, to music, to literary, to... Well, you name it, we represent it."

"I see. I prefer more classic fare than the latest thing."

"Oh, well, too bad, Mr. Banner. Say, can I call ya Jakie?"

"No."

"Thanks, Jakie. You see, I have this problem."

"Really?"

"Right now I'm working for Evangelyne Martini. You heard of her? She's great! This kid can sing, act, dance. She'll be the next great pop sensation."

"Aren't they all?"

"She's about to go on her first live performance tour. We need someone who can get her from show to show."

"Why doesn't she just tour with the band?"

"Aw, c'mon, Jakie. Talent never slums with the hired help. Besides, the media will be all over the main tour ship. It'd be much easier to control access if she's on another ship." Sid glanced around the room. "The look is okay. Evvie could do her interviews from here."

"Interviews?"

Sid raised his hands. "Strictly over the air stuff. You won't have to worry about anyone boarding."

"Okay. So all I have to do is get this 'Evvie' from one show to the next. For how long?"

"Well, we're still booking shows, but no more than three standard months. Three and a half at the most."

"And it will be just her? No family?"

"Her folks have split up again. It'd be bad to have either one, and if they both come they'll be fighting. Evvie doesn't need that, not on her first tour."

"No friends? No entourage?"

"Her friends will meet her at some of the gigs, but they can't drop their lives for three months. And we've got a directive from top brass to keep costs down on this first tour. Anything else?"

"No."

"You available?"

Sid's offer wasn't quite what Jake was expecting. But the spacer knew money when he saw it, so he decided to see if there would be real pay or hot air. His face became a mask of worry. "I don't know. I've got heavy debts to Questor. They aren't letting me leave."

"Hey, no problem!" Sid yanked out a small black box from a pocket. He pulled an ear plug from it, put it in his ear, and tapped a button on the box. "Hey, Nancy? Sid here. I got a fella who can help us with Evvie, but he's got some high-grav debt. Name? What was that name again?"

"Jake. Bonner."

"Jake Bonner, Nans. Huh. Hold on." He turned to Jake. "We'll bail you out, Jakie, but I need to get your okay on the legal stuff."

"Fine."

Sid disconnected the earpiece from his perscomp, tapped the screen a few times, then handed it to Jake. "Okay, that one is the independent contractor agreement spelling out the terms we've discussed. You're familiar with those, right?"

"No problem. Odin?"

"Who's Odin?"

"My ship's computer. Odin?"

"Scanning the contract, Jake. Nothing out of the ordinary."

"Wow," Sid said, "that's some computer. He available for license?"

"No," Jake answered. He scrolled to the end of the digital contract and signed the screen on the "dotted line." He started to hand the device back to Sid when Sid pointed to it.

"The next one is nondisclosure agreement covering the tour."

"Fine." Jake signed.

"Next is a nondisclosure about any songs Evvie composes, in part or in full, while she's on board your ship."

Jake signed.

"After that is the guarantee that you have insurance. Then you need to sign the insurance claim waivers for claims against us, from losses to acts beyond our control, and from losses you might incur while you work for us but aren't related to said work."

"Is that it?"

"No. Now you need to sign the agreement that you won't try to harm Evvie physically or mentally. Then you have to agree not to sell any information you gather about Evvie while working for us for a period of at least five years. We also need you to agree not to allow unauthorized media access to Evvie. Oh, we'll download the interview schedule. We also need you to agree not to allow any personal access to Evvie without getting our approval."

"Fine. Anything else?"

"Yeah. That last one is your agreement not to work for any other celebrity not represented by my firm while you work for us. You'll note that we reserve the right to request your services for celebrities that we do manage while under contract for us. Don't worry, there's no renewal option."

Jake signed the final contract. He handed the device to Sid. "Odin," he asked, "have I signed my life away?"

"Every contract was fair and ethical."

"Thank you."

"Yeah, thanks, Jake." Sid reattached the earpiece to the machine and tapped the screen twice. "Nancy? Okay, authorize payment on those debts. Done? Okay, kiddo, thanks. Be in touch." He took out the plug and put the communicator back in his pocket. "There, Jakie, all taken care of."

"Thanks. When do we start?"

"I'll download all the relevant data to you, then bring Evvie over." Sid grabbed Jake's hand and shook it again. "It'll be great working with ya, Jakie."

As soon as the agent was gone Odin said, "Happy to have been of assistance, Jake. Oh, by the way, Antioch Two appears to be a late stop on Miss Martini's tour."

"Interesting coincidence. That is a coincidence, right, Odin?"

"I would never do anything that underhanded. As it happens, the leader of Antioch Two is a fan of Miss Martini."

Jake shook his head. "I hate him already," he said.

Two
Off To A Bad Start

Jake rose early the next day to be ready to start his employment under Sid Kraft and Evangelyne Martini. Not that he was looking forward to the work. He didn't like Sid from the instant he stepped on the ship, and he was almost certain that he wouldn't like the pop star either. But they had erased his debts and were going to pay him well for his services. Jake felt that at the very least he ought to be appreciative, and that meant getting up early and appearing to be committed to his new employers.

As it happened, Jake's effort was slightly wasted on them. It was midmorning before Sid contacted Jake to inform him that "Evvie would be along any moment." About an hour's worth of moments passed between that call and the actual request to enter Skuld. Jake walked down the corridor to the airlock to meet them in person.

Sid was the first to come through the entrance. "Great to see ya again, Jakie."

"Thanks."

"Now, I'd like ya to meet the star of the hour, the sensation the whole family can enjoy, Miss Evangelyne Martini."

Miss Evangelyne Martini appeared to Jake's eyes to be a girl of nineteen going on sixteen. She was short, maybe five-one if she was lucky, with body hovering between average and petite. She had an inoffensive face, light brown eyes, and an almost-earnest smile. She was clearly a brunette, but had dyed her hair blonde, then dyed strands of it yellow and light orange. Her clothing was brightly colored, with yellow the predominant shade, and was styled "good girl" with a few hints of "young woman."

Her look meshed with what Jake knew about her past. She was the only child of parents who had married, divorced, remarried, and were now separated. She'd shown talents for dancing and singing at a very early age along with a great deal of personal charm. At the age of ten she became the star of *Captain Sandy*, a kid's show, entertainment computer program, and info-site that was popular on a half-dozen worlds for about a year and a half. At thirteen she was cast in HeritageNet's *Nice Ice Club*, an entertainment show that doubled as promotion for the corporation's indoor fun center chain.

It was there that "Evvie" began to emerge as a celebrity in her own right. Within a year she became the show's star performer. Sites popped up devoted to her, media outlets began to pay attention to her offstage life, and her mother hooked up with a celebrity career advisor. Luckily for Evvie, her mother, and the advisor, one of the other, much prettier girls on the show became jealous of the rising teen star. The "good girl" persona being crafted for Evvie fit the situation almost too perfectly. When she was more-or-less forced out after a three-year run, fame was practically kicking down her door.

The next step in Evvie's ascent came a year after she left *Nice Ice*. At seventeen she released her first music single, which quickly jumped into the top fifty. Her third release went into the top ten. Now, two years later, she'd had eight hits with her current release at Number One. These hits were to be combined with a couple songs that hadn't charted and a few that were planned for release , as Jake understood it, to make up enough material for this live performance tour.

In short, Jake thought, *she's the typical "nice girl" pop singer on the standard celebrity track.*

With that Jake returned to the present and the guest coming aboard Skuld. "Miss Martini,"he said, "I'm Jake Bonner. Welcome aboard my ship." He offered his right hand.

She shook it once, more politely than his greeting had been. "Thanks." She stepped around Sid through the airlock and into the corridor. She turned to Sid. "You coming?"

"Sorry, Evvie. I'll be traveling with the crew." He smiled to Jake. "Gotta keep the natives happy and the ball rolling, y'know."

"Sure."

"Well, Jakie, you take care of our little supernova. Evvie, I'll see ya tomorrow on Angelus Two."

"See you then. I'll call if something comes up before."

She stood up on the tips of her toes to kiss Sid on the cheek. He kissed the air next to her face. He gave Jake a decidedly nonmilitary salute, then turned headed back the connecting walkway to the space station. Jake tapped a keypad on the corridor wall next to the airlock doorway. The airlock closed, followed a second later by the doorway.

"All right, Miss Martini," Jake began.

"Call me Evvie."

"Okay, Evvie. It's customary for the captain of a ship to give a new passenger a tour. Unfortunately, there's not much to see. But it all works well. You're in one of the best ships in known space."

"Hey, I always like the best, Jakie."

"It's Jake."

"Oh."

Jake pointed to their left. Two meters beyond the open corridor ended in a closed doorway. "That way is the heart of this ship. There's an armory, the main power room, the jump drive housing, and at the end is the sublight drive."

"Armory?" Evvie gave Jake a nervous expression, as if he was suddenly something to be afraid of.

"Skuld was built as a military vessel." He worked hard to sound reassuring. "Don't worry, there's only a pair of blaster pistols, one laser rifle, an EVA suit, and some miscellaneous gadgets in there. It's all legal for a private starship. I don't collect weapons, if that's what you're thinking."

"Okay."

Jake waved at door opposite and to the right of the airlock entrance. "That room is the auxiliary bridge." He started walking up the corridor with Evvie a few steps behind him. "Next is the communications and sensor room, and next to that is a teleport. It's completely reliable. We can teleport you down anywhere; you never have to go through airlocks. I am pleased to say that this ship is the first private vessel to have a working teleport."

"Okay." Evvie waved at the sole door on the other side of the corridor. "What's in there?"

Jake tapped a keypad to open the door. The empty room was painted a translucent black. "The holoroom," he said casually.

"Oh, stars! You have a holoroom?" Evvie marched into the room. She looked around in obvious awe. An honest smile burst onto her face. "This is so cool! Y'know, I begged my mom to get us one when we moved into our new house, but she didn't want to put down the creds until after the tour. This is beyond spiff, Jake."

He walked in after her. "Thanks."

"It's not very deep, though. Well, maybe it's as wide as my stage will be."

"It wasn't designed for recreation, Evvie. As I said, this was to

13

be a military ship. Specifically, this ship was built to conduct espionage missions. Fortunately for me the original owners decided to abandon the experiment. Anyway, I have taken the time and expense to download some appropriate sims for this room." He waved the other end of the room. "And over there are two immersion suits. Full body experience, if you have a sim you can't play out in here."

"Oh, this is so spiff. I'm glad Sid hired you."

"Thanks. Can we continue?"

"Yeah, okay."

Jake led her out of the room. He tapped the keypad to close the door. He led her up the corridor past four closed doors on both sides. "Ignore these rooms. They're vacant, or being used for storage." He stopped at the fifth pair of doors "This is my room," he said, pointing left, "and yours is here," he finished, pointing right.

"Can I see my room?"

"Sure." He opened the door.

The room was basic, but not as sparse one might expect from a former military starship. There was an actual bed, drawers, private bathroom, walk-in closet, food replicator, in-room entertainment screen, and even carpet on the floor. The decor was nonexistent; the walls were painted gray, the sheets were navy blue, the carpet a clean off-white.

"It's ugly," was all Evvie could say.

"It's not that bad," Jake replied.

"The walls self-coloring?"

"Militaries don't have a need for them, and I can't afford the retrofit."

"I'd pay for it."

"And who would pay to have it removed? Evvie, I don't make it my business to fly pop stars across human space."

"I can tell."

"Look, you can put up any pictures or holos you want. I'll let you temporarily replace the sheets. Besides, it's not like you're permanently moving here. A few months, and you'll be back to your stylish life at home."

"I guess." She took a few steps inside. "That closet doesn't look big enough."

"We've got eight other rooms for storage, if you need them."

"Oh, okay. Maybe two will be enough. Or three."

"Fine." He motioned to her. "One more stop."

She left the room. Jake led her through the open entranceway. "This is the main room. Couch, two chairs, big screen. Up there, where the two seats are, that's the bridge." He motioned for her to sit down across from him in the couch. He sat down in the chair next to the screen. "It's small ship, but but its gets the job done."

"How much did it cost? I might like to buy one these for crusin'. Modify the bedrooms, of course."

"It was free."

"It was found property," Odin said.

"Uh, what does it... er, what do you mean, uh..."

"Odin. And since I am sentient, and my namesake a male Norse god, you may refer to me as 'he' or 'him.' What I mean is, Jake did not purchase this ship. He found this ship in an uninhabited region of space with myself and my systems deactivated. He was kind enough to reactivate me.

"You see, Miss Martini, as Jake said before I was created with the purpose of conducting espionage missions for the government that built me. However, once I gained sentience, I noted the inherent moral complications of such activities. Furthermore, the officers sent to command this ship had an unpleasant habit of giving orders that were, shall I say, much less than perfectly clear."

"To make a long story short," Jake said, "Odin was so uncooperative that the military of Svedal Three decided it was cheaper and easier to abandon this ship than destroy it. As it happened, they left Skuld in an unsettled region of space. I found the ship while fleeing an enemy of a former employer. I came on board, reactivated Odin, and took possession."

"I displayed my appreciation for Jake's actions by allowing him to remain on board, to be a little more precise."

"The ownership documents have my name on them, Odin," Jake said over his shoulder, "not yours. This ship is my property."

"A sentient being cannot own another. It is only because I like you that I do not press that question."

"That, and the fact that without a human earning income, there isn't a whole lot you could do on your own." Jake waited for Odin to address his point. When Odin said nothing, Jake turned back to Evvie. "It's a sensitive subject for him. Now, do you have any questions?'"

"How many other bedrooms are there? Could I get my friends on board?"

"Those eight other rooms , the ones we're using for storage. None of them have furniture in them. A little fire sale to pay off some debts a year ago."

She looked slightly crushed. "Oh. You have any good interactives in that holoroom?"

"You'd have to check yourself. If you have any favorites, you're free to upload them into our d-base. Odin can program sims himself, if there's something special or specific you're looking for."

"Spiff."

"Anything else?"

She thought for an instant, then shook her head. "Nope." She stood up. " I guess you can, what, beam my stuff up."

"Yeah. That's all you want to know. You don't have any questions about the security systems, the teleport, how to operate anything,..."

"Nope. If I can't figure it out it isn't important. C'mon, Jake, I wanna get my stuff onboard and unpack." Without waiting for him to stand up she jogged off to the teleport room.

Jake stood and shook his head. "Odin, I have a bad feeling about this."

"My immediate analysis indicates you may be right. I shall raise all the emergency protocols to higher levels in my memory directory."

***

Bringing Evvie's luggage onto the ship was easy. Jake simply put on a teleport bracelet, had Odin transport him to where her bags were, and beamed back until all six were aboard. Evvie decided to eat lunch while she unpacked. Jake didn't need her to urge him to leave her alone. He was happy to let her dig through her clothes and personal belongs; he feared seeing them might only make him crazy.

He ate his lunch on the bridge. He had other business to attend to, namely to find out what Odin had discovered about the planet his other employers called home. As he ate the screen in front of him came alive.

The first image was a digitized rendering of a solar system. "The Antioch system is comparatively small," Odin began. "There are only five worlds in the system, including one gas giant and one habitable world, Antioch Two. Planetary surveys indicate that the innermost world and the third world have limited wealth potential, mainly in minerals used in various manufacturing processes. The fourth world may have greater potential, but it has an eccentric orbit and has no real atmosphere."

Next came a rotating three-dimensional view of Antioch Two from space. "The second world does have a habitable atmosphere. It lies point-nine-seven AU from its star, leading to a warmer atmosphere than Earth standard. Science surveys did find native life, but evolution here is proceeding at a slow pace due to the warm conditions."

The world that Odin showed Jake was a two-color planet known among spacers as a "wet rockball." This was because Antioch Two had three continents and many islands, with the rest of its surface covered by water. The land areas consisted of rocky mountain chains, rocky deserts, and rocky coastlines. It was the sort of world that only a mineralogist could love.

Well, so much for appealing to natural beauty to stop this dictator, Jake thought.

After half a minute the rotating view of the planet stopped. The world then filled the small screen until an aerial view of a habitation dome appeared. The camera movement didn't stop until the dome took up a screen area of ten centimeters. "All the human residents of Antioch Two live in this dome. It is located in the northern hemisphere in a standard desert environment. This location is the closest to the most productive gold and silver veins. It is the second such dome constructed; the first was removed seventy years ago due to mines in that area being fully exploited."

"How long will it take to deplete these veins?" Jake asked.

"At the present pace, roughly twenty years."

"And the fact that native life exists never deterred mining?"

"Apparently not. I have accessed projections that don't suggest any higher lifeforms will evolve on Antioch Two."

"How reliable are they? Or were they corporately funded?"

"Their pedigree is reasonably solid. The most unfavorable projection, as far as mineral exploitation, estimates that intelligent life might evolve in a seven to ten billion year timespan. The others state the probability of such an evolutionary course at fifty percent or less."

"All right. Tell me more about that dome."

"Of course." The dome image was replaced on the screen with a surface map. "The dome is located within three kilometers of a substantial river. That river is dammed to provide for both water and power."

"No fuel cells?"

"Any native natural gas or other such sources of energy are extremely small. There is geothermal activity on the planet, but not where the mineral veins are located. The aqua-cells are not as efficient, but seem to provide adequate power for planetary needs. All other standard facilities, such as water reclamation and pollution conversion, are present."

Jake looked at the image of the dome for a few moments. The exterior appeared fairly standard. It was a gray structure spiderwebbed by black support beams and silvery panel joints. "Dome" was the common name for such structures, but in reality it was a cylinder capped by an actual dome. The cylinder appeared to be about five or six stories tall, with the dome an additional story. It resembled every other habitation dome on every other rough planet that Jake had been to or heard about.

"All very above board, it seems," he said at length.

"'Seems' being the operative word, Jake. I cannot locate any detailed data on Antioch Two, such as the types of systems used, exact mineral output, or even if the world has been inspected for health and safety violations."

Jake frowned and shook his head. "Odin, that doesn't make sense."

"Ordinarily, you would be correct."

"But?"

"But it seems that in this particular case, you are incorrect. Interstellar law does exempt privately-owned exploited worlds from most regulation."

"But that law is supposed to cover asteroids and uninhabitable worlds."

"So is Antioch Two. It appears from my investigation that the world is the personal property of Sordius Maxis."

Jake leaned back in his chair. It took him a moment to digest what Odin had just said. "One man owns one of the richest worlds in human space?"

"That appears to be the case."

"How could that be? How could one man own a planet? How could any corporation have let this gem slip away?"

"I have no information at this time, Jake. It appears that Maxis, or possibly his father, found the ideal loophole."

"Or pulled off the con of the millennium."

Jake suddenly smiled. "Which means beating him is going to be beating a conman. I may actually enjoy this after all."

"Happy to have been of service," Odin responded, with just a touch of digitized sincerity.

***

As the day came to an end, Jake stretched out on the couch. He rubbed his hands together in anticipation. "It all comes down to this," he said quietly.

"Did you say something?"

Jake turned. Evvie was standing in the entranceway connecting the main control room to the rest of the ship. She was dressed in a peach nightshirt and lavender pajama bottoms, and on her feet were fat bunny slippers. Jake wasn't quite sure what to make of the sight. From what little he knew of her, the outfit almost seemed believable.

But on the other hand, he thought, *she looks too much like a teen actress from a bad comedy series dressed for a bedroom scene.*

"Did you say something to me?" she asked again.

"Uh, no. The finals for *RoboJoust* are just about to come on."

"*RoboJoust?*" Evvie frowned. "Isn't that show for lonely loser geeks?"

"I think it's time for you to go to bed," Jake snapped.

"And a good night to you, too, Jake." She shook her head, turned, and wandered back to her room.

"Screen, on."

"Volume?" Odin asked.

Jake sucked in an angry breath. *Damn, but I am tempted.*

"Medium low," he answered, "just this once."

The screen came alive. The first image to flash on was that of an oversized old-fashioned circuit board painted gold. The "board" sat at a tilt, and rotated on a pedestal. An unseen male voice came up to set the stage.

"This is the Motherboard of Victory," it said, "long a symbol of the nastiest, most vicious, and most triumphant robot combatant of the season. Tonight, live, you will see which 'bot team gets to claim the Motherboard. It's time for the RoboJoust season finals!"

The image of the "trophy" was replaced by inset images of small armed and armored vehicles racing into each other on grass and on dirt. Some crashed into bushes, while others were pushed into tiny ponds. At least one unfortunate machine that had somehow gotten airborne had its underbelly slammed into by an opponent and was sent tumbling. Finally the graphic *RoboJoust* was projected over the images of destruction. The opening ended with the word "Finals!" in a stencil font racing in from one corner to stop under the word "RoboJoust."

Jake let out an eager breath. He had become a fan of *RoboJoust* a few years ago when, during some downtime on another job, he happened across a broadcast. It hooked him almost instantly. On a gut level he could appreciate the combat and carnage, but the cleverness of design and the strategies of the bot owners also appealed to him. It was the one sport that could hold his interest for more than a few moments.

Jake was not quite a typical viewer of *RoboJoust*. The main audience were men from five to ten years younger than him. They were either still in college or just starting careers in astronomical engineering, programming, or some other highly technical field. But Jake's strong interest was shared by most of the audience. Since *RoboJoust* had been created about a decade ago, every measuring method showed that its audience consistently tuned in every week. Few advertisers had yet discovered it, but those that had appreciated it as much as the audience did. That audience, like Jake, was tuned in especially intensely to this broadcast. After fifteen weeks of local matches and a week each of quarterfinals and semifinals, the RoboJoust season came to end with the finals.

That was made abundantly clear by the two hosts of *RoboJoust*, Bill Martin and Dinesh Ral. Martin, a stocky man in his early thirties with cropped black hair and an easy smile, was the first to speak once the opening was over. "Yes, people, tonight is the night for fighting bots," he said. "In the words of the ancient gods of sportscasting, it all comes down to this."

The camera view shifted to Ral, a slim man in his late thirties. He was dressed more formally than Martin, but no less enthusiastic.

"Bill, you know your history," he said, nodding his head. "That's correct, fans of robot destruction. Fifteen matches, the quarters, and the semis have brought us to this night."

"And it is a very good night here at West Port Joust Park. We're back in the small city of Westport on Vandalia Three. West Port Park was selected at the start of this season to host this year's finals. And now, the best teams and their bots have ended their jumps here to see who gets the Motherboard, and who gets a kick in the ass."

As Martin spoke the image shifted from the *RoboJoust* studio to the joust park. The "combat area" wasn't much on the face of it. It was an open square, fifteen meters by fifteen, with a tiny pond to one side; a bush well to the right of the pond; a mound opposite that bush; another bush to the right and ahead of it; and a meter long ditch a few centimeters deep in the center. But in RoboJoust terms, it was the ideal spot to hold the finals. Every legal hazard was in the combat area, and none were too difficult for the combatants to deal with if they were smart. It was a balanced arena, unlike other parks where one hazard or the other might dominate. And except for the ditch the hazards were to the sides, leaving more space for the robotic vehicles to slug it out.

Finally the image of the park was replaced by a two-shot of Martin and Ral. "So, my friend," Martin asked, "what's our first finals match, and who will be knocking metal?"

"Bill, up first is the middleweight final. It pits Slayer and Team Warp against Tornado and Team Master."

The two-shot was replaced by a picture of a sandy-haired man with a trim beard in his late twenties. "Team Warp consists of Bran Murphee, who not only drives but also does all his own maintenance. This is just his second season competing in *RoboJoust*. He's come a long way in so short a time."

That was a sentiment Jake could agree with. As far as Jake knew, Murphee had been a fan of *RoboJoust* from the start. Just over two years ago Murphee decided to stop watching and join in. He pooled his own savings with an investment from a sci-fi shop on his home world and constructed his first entry, a lightweight robot called "Dark Knight."

Murphee didn't attract much attention early in his first season of competition. Since the second season fans of RoboJoust had gotten up from their chairs and entered robots. But as that season went along Murphee's profile rose. He beat a semifinalist from the year before, held his own against a quarterfinalist, and ended the season with an 8-7 record.

This season Murphee went on a tear. He scored twelve wins, and took out three of his opponents before time ran out. Slayer was not knocked out once, and two of the three losses were strictly based on the points awarded by the judges. Murphee had become a new fan favorite, and there was plenty of cheering for him among the spectators and the audience, Jake included.

Murphee's picture on Jake's screen was replaced by one of his robot. "Slayer is a four-wheeled killer. It's turtle-like shell has made it hard to beat, and its retractable spike has stabbed twelve opponents to death. In its first season, Slayer has a solid three K-O's."

The next image on the screen was of a mustachioed man pushing forty with thinning dark hair and a gap-toothed smile. "Team Master is led by longtime champion Carlo Kidder. Interestingly, this is only the second time Carlo has had a bot even make it into the middleweight finals. That was four seasons ago, and that bot, King Rat, was shredded in the semifinal match."

Kidder's image was then replaced by that of his robot. "Tornado is a six-wheeled monstrosity with a top-mounted spinning blade. It's racked up an impressive five knockouts this season, with one coming in the quarterfinal. But don't let its bulk fool you; early this season Tornado used its weight to push Flash into hazards when its blade went buggy."

In Jake's mind the match was not a simple good-versus-evil showdown. While he liked Murphee, he didn't hate Carlo Kidder. Kidder was nice guy, a clever tinkerer, and a decent competitor. He rarely gloated when he won, not even running one of his robots on a victory lap or dance. Jake couldn't remember when Kidder had not been gracious in defeat, and in fact the only lapse had occurred during his first year of competition due to a questionable awarding of points. If it had been against anyone else and with any other bot, Jake would have cheered for Kidder.

The only obstacle was Kidder's bot. Jake found Tornado to be one butt-ugly machine. It's six wheels seemed ungainly, and the decoration on the spinning blade hurt his eyes when it was in action. It didn't help to see sponsor signs plastered on all four sides, each of which was carefully restored if damaged. Finally, the spinning blade was about as subtle as a brick. All in all, Jake hoped that Slayer would spear Tornado.

The image on the screen in front of him shifted back from Tornado to a two-shot of commentators Martin and Ral. "Okay, Dinesh, put yours cards on the table. Who do you like in this one?"

"Well, Bill, Slayer's fast and aggressive, but Tornado is big and powerful. Add to that Carlo Kidder's experience, and I think Tornado has to be the favorite."

"I gotta disagree with you, my friend. Murphee's the best driver in his division, and he's fought here before this season. I think Slayer has a chance."

"Okay. No matter what, it should be a good match."

"No doubt about that. Well, it looks like the introductions to the crowd are over. Let's go down to the field and find out who's going to be this season's middleweight champ."

The image on the screen shifted from the studio to the arena. A countdown clock ticked off seconds in negative numbers. When the clock reached "0:00:00," a loud buzzer sounded. The match was underway. While their faces weren't on the screen, the voices of Martin and Ral narrated the action on the screen.

"And Slayer's moving out fast and heading straight for Tornado!"

"Murphee's aggressive, no doubt about it."

"And wham! Slayer draws first blood before Tornado's blade has time to get going. That's a smart move on Murphee's part, getting in blow before that blade is up at full speed."

"Now we'll see if Tornado will let that hit go unanswered."

"Both bots are moving around. Slayer's trying to stay away from that blade. Tornado's lumbering to get into a position that limits Slayer's options."

"No one's going to take any risks at this point. There's three minutes to go. Plenty of time to get the job done."

"Looks like Tornado's trying to get up on that mound, maybe get some momentum coming down."

"Or maybe lure Slayer into a trap. It's rounded shell would be much easier to damage if Tornado hit it at an angle."

"And there goes Slayer! Maybe Murphee... Bam! Slayer nails one of Tornado's tires! Oh, man, that Murphee's got guts."

"Luckily Tornado has six wheels. That's not going to be fatal damage."

"But a hit is a hit, and Slayer has two. So far Tornado is just spinning air. It's no F6 in this match. Kidder's got to get in there now."

"Kidder said earlier this season that he wanted Tornado to have some heft to deal with bots lower than the blade. But here the heft is just slowing him down."

"Oh, but now he's pissed. Even with one tire spiked, he's getting Tornado moving. He wants to get in there and smack Slayer around."

"But Slayer isn't taking the bait this time. He's backing away, and keeping the end with the spike facing Tornado."

"That's a very good strategy on Murphee's part. Hey! Slayer's getting close to the water."

"Oh, and he turns just in time."

"Oh, my, Tornado isn't going to!"

"No, way, pal! Ow! Tornado hits the water hazard! It was just a glancing blow, but that still costs him. And your bot Tornado is in a pretty deep hole right now."

"But Kidder is experienced enough that he can still get out, if he can just get in close."

"But you can bet your jump drive that Murphee ain't gonna risk it now. He's out ahead, and as long as he doesn't make any mistakes he won't be giving up his lead.

"Now, Slayer's stopped behind the mound. He moves forward, moves back. Oh, man, he's saying, 'Hey, come here, Tornado. I gotta spike I wanna drive into you.' Tornado's moving in slowly. Kidder's trying to find a way in."

"One minute left."

"Kidder's still trying to get in. I think that lost tire might also be slowing him down. Ho, there he goes! Oh, and Slayer darts around the other side of the mound and into the open! He was stalling for time."

"Oh, my, no!"

"And Kidder can't get Tornado turned around enough to make another run at Slayer. He's trying, he's trying, there he goes. Now Tornado means business."

"Just one good hit, that's all he needs."

"And there goes Slayer again! This time he's camping in front of the ditch. Oh, man, if Tornado makes a run now, he could pull it off."

"There he goes."

"And Slayer pulls out again! Kidder had better..."

"Oh, no!"

"Thump! Tornado hits the ditch with twenty seconds left."

"There's Slayer!"

"Bam! That's one. That's two! And now Slayer pulls back from Tornado. Murphee knows he's got it won. Lookit, a victory dance from Slayer. And that's the match! Slayer in an upset! The veteran Carlo Kidder, defeated by the newbie Bran Murphee, and by a landslide. Tornado was sucking vacuum, while Slayer inflicted four unanswered hits."

"The judges' votes are in. Slayer nine, Tornado null."

"Well, you saw it here. The first match was an upset. We'll be back with the awarding of the Motherboard, the hit of the match, and the heavyweight final, right after this shameless begging from the megacorps that deign to support us. Don't you change your feed."

The image on the screen froze. "Jake," Odin said, "I hate to interrupt you, but tomorrow's schedule..."

"Will be a long one, I know. Save the rest for later viewing. It will give me something good to watch during Evvie's concert."

"Done."

Jake stood, stretched his arms, then bent over a few times. He rubbed his neck with his right hand. He let out a breath, then started walking to his bedroom.

Robert Collins

**Three
A Clause For Everything**

Jake had been watching Evvie's first "performance" for less than half an hour when boredom overtook him. The songs had melded together in an amorphous mass of up-tempo pleasantries. Anonymous and toned male and female dancers were moving in endless synchronization. Holographic images were merging into brightly-colored blobs.

With the right pharmaceuticals, he thought, *this might make for a nice little buzz.*

Jake could not escape the images on the screen so easily. He had to maintain a watch on the "concert" so as to properly perform his job. Sid had provided him with the list of songs Evvie would perform, so Jake would know when the show was over. It was a good gesture, but it also gave Jake more information on her career than he'd ever wanted.

The first song of her concert was "Sweet Kisses and Sour Grapes." It was her seventh hit and by far her most popular song. If pressed Jake would admit that the tune had some merit. It told the story of a girl who wanted a boy but was rejected by him; while she dreamed of giving him "sweet kisses," she wondered if he was better in her dreams than in reality. It had some spark of imagination, but it was also entirely predictable.

The second slot in the concert was held by her first hit as a pop singer, "Baby Move Your Groove." It was like every other teen dance hit Jake had ever known of, and naturally was Evvie's second most-popular hit. The song was followed by two upcoming releases, the cloying "Toys and Candy" and the nauseating "That Famous Little Girl." Jake suspected that if those two became hits, they'd switch places in the lineup with the first song.

Following those two were a handful of ballads, the first of which was Evvie's third hit, "Diary Of My Heart." After that came "I'm Looking His Way" and "That Should Be Us." Each was full of the teen love angst that had been a staple of the genre since time immemorial. When he heard each for the first time, Jake had to

26

struggle from bursting out with laughter. The songs contained the sort of unintentional humor that the genre had become notorious for early in the Twenty-First Century. He felt their only redeeming value was that Evvie sang them without the annoying vocal effects that cluttered up her other singles.

The ballad break was followed by the most cluttered of those other songs, the assertive dance hit "Back On My Feet." After that was "(Don't Be A) Silly Boy," and then to end the show came "Hot & Cold Love." The second-to-last song in the lineup was the one that truly baffled Jake. It was simultaneously an up-tempo dance song, a flirty come-on, and a female empowerment tune. It managed to be trite one moment and ponderous the next. Yet despite what seemed to be obvious flaws, it was the song most popular with Evvie's diehard fans.

It must be one of those songs, Jake concluded, *that seems brilliant at fifteen and pointless at twenty. That is the only possible explanation for it.*

Partway through the concert Jake began to wonder if it might be a good idea to hand off the monitoring task to Odin. He'd just about decided to make the request when Odin said to him, "Jake, I have a transmission request from Antioch Two. Shall I patch it through?"

"God, yes. Anything's better than this. Oh, and keep watch on the show for me, please. Let me know when Evvie gets near the end."

"Certainly. Stand by."

The concert image became a tiny and silent box in the upper left corner of the screen. Daniel Rosen's face appeared on the rest. He wore an expression of stern determination. In any other context, someone might have asked him what he'd eaten that was making him frown so much. Jake himself wondered if he might have to amend his last sentence.

"Robin Hood, this is Friar Tuck," Daniel began.

Jake glanced up at the ceiling and rolled his eyes. He exhaled, then asked, "Odin, you are scrambling this, I hope?"

"Of course."

Jake's gaze returned to Daniel. "Mister Rosen, there is no need for code words or phrases. My ship is capable of securing my communication to you, and yours to me. So, please, can we speak without the melodramatics?"

Daniel's face fell slightly. "Oh, yes, sure."

Jake had the odd suspicion come over him that Rosen had taken a great deal of time to devise a code for their communications, and that he was disappointed that all of his effort would be in vain. Of course, had Rosen pondered the matter a bit more deeply, it would have probably occurred to him that scrambling was much easier these days than speaking in code. Jake began to hope that Rosen would not be so oblivious as their partnership continued.

"Now, Daniel, what's on your mind?"

"Um, well, Clarissa and I have returned home, and we were just wondering, well, is there anything we ought to be doing?"

"Doing? Like what?"

"Well, organizing, maybe."

"Organizing?" *If it wasn't for the wealth potential, I would not do this.*

"Tell me," Jake asked slowly, "what precisely do you intend to organize?"

"A resistance," Daniel replied, more a question than a statement.

"And what do you think you will do with this resistance?"

"Uh, resist?"

"You can't define a word with that word. What are you going to do?"

Daniel started to answer, then hesitated. Possible replies seemed to fly into his mind at light speed and exit just as fast. After almost a minute of this he finally said, "Protest, undermine Maxis' rule, prepare for you. Y'know, that sort of thing."

"I won't be able to assist you in person for about three standard months, Mister Rosen. Now if your organizing and resisting gets you or your wife or the both of you arrested, I will have a very hard time contacting you. It will be even harder for us to transact business. Correct?"

"Yeah, I guess so."

"For me to give you any help, you are going to have to be able to keep in touch with me."

"But, what about...?"

"Listen, stop getting your ideas from ancient movies. You don't organize a resistance when people are unhappy. You organize when they're fed up and ready to act. If your people were that angry you wouldn't need me to help get the ball rolling, right?"

"Well, I suppose,..."

"Trust me. For now all you and your wife need to do is feed me data. Put together information on your work routines, the layout of your domes, the names of your friends, any stray fact that might be of use to me. Even the parents of your security guards."

"We don't have guards. We have guard-bots."

"Then send me their make and model numbers. Just gather the data and keep an eye on how people feel. Can you do that, and only that?"

"We can."

"Good. Now, next time I will call you. Don't call me unless it's urgent. Are we all synced up, Daniel?"

"Sure."

"Great. Start gathering, and I'll call back in a few days, probably at this same time. Goodbye."

Daniel's face disappeared, and the concert transmission enlarged to fill the screen again. Jake tapped a few keypads on one of the bridge panels. He might have to watch Evvie at work, but that didn't mean he had to listen to her as well. After some searching he was able to find an acceptable substitute, and the play-by-play of a *RoboJoust* game in the Earth Alliance League drifted through the cabin.

"Odin, if the Rosens ask you for any subversive literature, don't indulge them without my approval."

"All right. Why?"

"Because knowing those two, they'll start talking to me in accents."

***

Every morning as Jake passed by the holoroom on his way to the bridge he heard awful noises. Musical instruments screeched and crowds cheered. On one particular morning, a week into his escort job, the noise was especially unpleasant. He decided to go inside the holo-room and try to put a stop to the abuse of his superb facilities.

Evvie was again using the room to rehearse her live show. The second day on board she had been able to program a stage show, her backup players and dancers, and the special effects. The third day she learned how to program the audience. They never booed, but then neither did the real crowds.

Jake almost felt himself drawn to the spectacle. It was like

29

passing by a starship disaster; you couldn't help but watch while the sight repelled you.

He had decided some time ago that Evvie wouldn't catch anyone's eye if you saw her as a normal young woman on the street. Her on-stage dress combined good-girl trendy with bad-girl trash. She sang with no accent, her dance routines were, well, "routine," and her concerts devoid of random acts of personality. It was this "averageness" that in reality was completely false and highly crafted, that put kept her in the long-established mold of a "teen pop singing sensation."

Jake struggled not to throw up his breakfast.

"Program, pause!" he snapped.

Evvie gave him a wide frown. "Why'd ya stop it?"

"Could you at least not play that... that... drivel so loud?"

"This isn't drizzle. This is good music!"

Jake felt his bile rise. "No, it is not. It's commercial garbage, designed to make money. Why do all you pop 'musicians' have to sing about the same old things? Why don't you sing about what happens in your life, instead of someone else's?"

"Don't take it so seriously," she replied with a shrug. "It's only music."

"Only music?"

"Well, yeah, isn't everything?"

"No! Is Beethoven's Ninth Symphony only music? Is the William Tell Overture only music? Is 'Let It Be' only music?"

Evvie blinked. "Was all that written by the same guy?"

"I can't believe this! You are a musical idiot!" Jake spun and stormed out of the room.

"I am not!" She followed him onto the bridge. "You just don't like that I'm popular."

"No. Popularity has nothing to do with it. It's about honesty, sincerity, having something new to say."

"No, you're just jealous." She glanced around. "Say, is it time for my interview?"

"Thirty-one minutes, ten seconds," Odin announced.

"Cool. Just enough time to get changed."

"Changed?" Jake asked. "You appear to be dressed as it is." For a pop star who sings crappy trash, he was desperate to add.

"This is one of my performance outfits," Evvie replied. Her

voice suggested that she was amazed that Jake hadn't noticed this fact. "I can't do an interview dressed like this. Especially since this one's with an older woman." She shook her head. "I'll be back in time." She turned and jogged off the bridge.

"It may interest you to know," Odin said, "that the interviewer in question is all of thirty-two."

"Odin, please. I am trying to keep down my breakfast."

***

As Evvie waited patiently for her interview to begin, Jake watched from his place by the ship controls and readouts. His first thought had been to switch places with her: he would watch from the lower part of the bridge while she sat in this seat. More thinking led him to decide that he didn't want Evvie near the controls; who knew pad she might tap in boredom or excitement.

It was just as well. Evvie immediately aimed for the couch in the lower section. "It won't look like I'm that isolated," she told him, "while keeping the freaks from peeking into my room."

Watching her now he was somewhat amazed that she didn't seem to be fidgeting, humming, or displaying any signs of nervousness. Even if she had experience with being interviewed, he believed that she ought to display some signal that she was waiting. A closer look at her face revealed to him the faint expression of concentration.

So that's it, he thought. *She's trying to remember what she wants to say. That explains everything.*

The interviewer had been glancing away from Evvie for the last several moments. She seemed to get some sort of signal off-camera. She nodded, turned to Evvie, and said, "Ready?"

"I'm ready."

The woman nodded again. "Hello, everyone," she began in a more perky tone, "this is Jen Carsten with PopRocksNet, and joining us is Evvie Martini. Hi, Evvie."

"Hi, Jen."

"You're out performing your songs live, I hear."

"Yeah. I've got enough tunes to make for a good hour-long show, and I wanted to say 'hi' to all my fans, so I'm hittin' space."

"Anything we can expect from your show, Evvie?"

"Lots of cool songs and a really spiff image show. Y'know, Jen, we shot a couple alternate clips for some of the songs, and I think we might give everyone who turns out a disc with those clips."

"Spiff songs and gifts for your fans? Evvie, that's so great."

"Yeah."

"So, how long are you out, and where are you going next?"

"I'll be on tour for three standard months yet. Tomorrow I'll be on New Paris. Uh, the next day I'll be on Caledonia, and then we go to Osage, Al-Haje, and Youngstown. For the whole tour list, ticket orders, PPV orders, and other cool stuff you can click to my infosite. Just type or speak 'Evvie.' I hope your viewers can check out the show."

"Let's hope so, Evvie. Good luck with your tour."

"Thanks!"

"We've been talking to Evvie Martini, a hot young star singing live for the next few months. I'll be back with more pop news, so don't click out." The interviewer waited a moment, then nodded to someone off-camera. An instant later she turned back to the subject of her interview. "Evvie, the piece is saved."

"Cool. When's it gonna run?"

"We'll run it on the quarter-hour for the next couple days, then every four hours for another three."

"That it?"

"We're done for now. Thanks for talking."

"Thank you."

"Well, that was deep," Jake said after the image faded. He rose from his seat and walked towards Evvie.

"What?"

"I think your interview clocked in at under two minutes. Maybe even a minute and a half."

"So?"

"It doesn't bother you that she didn't ask you about your songs. That the whole thing was hype and fluff."

Evvie shook her head. "No." She stood up and turned to leave.

"No?"

She turned to face him. "It was just a promo interview."

"Gee, I didn't know their job was to promote you."

"Of course, silly. What's the whole point of being interviewed if it doesn't boost sales and turnout?"

"Oh, I don't know. Maybe to show people who you really are. Maybe to elicit actual information. A real answer might be nice."

"Hey, I'm not in any scandal. I don't need to deal with that.

Look, I need to go rehearse." Without waiting for Jake to respond, Evvie turned and walked off the bridge.

"Oh, the depths we have fallen to," he said once she was gone.

"I don't believe 'depth' is quite appropriate, Jake," Odin observed.

***

"Odin, I think now would be good time to contact the Rosens."

"If you say so."

Evvie's concert was at the halfway mark. There was a risk in attempting to make contact, mainly that Jake might be late in picking her up and she might then get suspicious. But four days had passed since Daniel had called. Jake thought more than enough time had passed for him to find out what Jake needed to know. He also didn't want to get the Rosens nervous by being out of touch for too long. Who knows what trouble they could get into if Jake didn't keep an eye on them.

Once again Daniel's image took over much of the screen. "Yes?" he asked calmly.

"I'm not interrupting anything, am I?" Jake wasn't certain, but Daniel appeared to be in pajamas.

"Oh, no. Our sleep cycle doesn't start for about twenty minutes."

"Sorry. We'll try to keep your local time in mind when we call. Any luck gathering the information I requested?"

"No problems. Most of it is stuff everyone knows."

"Well, time is short for both of us. Start with the basics."

"Okay. Our main dome has six levels. Maxis and his cronies live up of the top level. Level two is where foremen and their families live. It's also where we have the sickbay, the schools, and the main cafeteria."

"Everyone eats there? At the same time?"

"Yes, but in shifts. I guess it's cheaper than building additional domes near the mines," he added with a slight sneer.

"Probably. Go on."

"The rest of the workers live on levels three, four, and five. Six is the bottom level, where the vehicles are stored. Everyone boards hover-buses there to ride to their workplaces."

"Okay, Daniel, that's a nice travelogue. How about some hard facts?"

"Like?"

"You say Maxis uses guardbots. Where are they controlled from? Where are they repaired?"

"We haven't yet found out where they're controlled, but we know that there's a maintenance shop on level six."

"Down there? Surely that's not the only shop. How well do you know the levels?"

"I know two through five pretty well. I don't think there's any more on six that we've missed. I've only been to the top level once. Clarissa has been there a few times."

Clarissa edged her face next to her husband's. "Hi, Mister Bonner."

"Clarissa? Anything to add?" Jake asked.

"Not really. I think there's a control room on the top level, but I don't know what's in there or how many people work there."

Jake exhaled. "Okay, let's take it from another angle. You've told me about the main dome. How many other domes are there?"

"One for the processing plant," Daniel answered, "one for waste reclamation, one for supply storage, and maybe seven or eight mines."

"The number of mines varies," Clarissa said. "One closed down a year ago, but crews are working on building two new ones."

"Okay." Jake paused for a moment to think. He could see the Rosens had some serious gaps in their knowledge. They knew nothing about the security systems. Their layout of the dome left some unused space, if he was right about his estimate of the dome's size.

Question is, he mused, *are they in a position to find out?*

"What do you two do?" he asked them. "What are your jobs?"

Brief expressions of shame crossed their faces before Daniel answered. "I'm the deputy foreman at the processing plant. Clarissa is crew chief at one of the mines."

"I see." *And I think I begin to understand why you want a revolution.* "Daniel, I think you're in a better position to ask questions than Clarissa. I'd like you to talk security with your boss. Now, you said you have a supply dome, correct?"

"That's right."

"That means all your food, water, major equipment, it all gets shipped in from off-world."

"Yes."

"Okay. Try in a roundabout way to ask your boss how crews of those off-world ships are kept from getting at any gold or silver. If he asks why you're asking, tell him there's a rumor going around about an off-worlder trying to pull a heist. You want some facts to dispel the rumors."

"I can do that."

"I'd also like both of you to keep your eyes open. Look for doors that don't seem to lead to anything. See where your supervisors go. Don't do any snooping, or ask anyone else questions. Got that?"

"Sure."

"One last thing. If you get some time, compile the history of your world as you know it, as well as a list of all the executives' names."

"Is that a file we have to store?" Clarissa asked. "Having something like that could get us in trouble."

Jake pondered the problem for an instant. "Can you download games?"

"From an approved list."

"Do you have very many?"

"No."

"Send us that list. Now." Jake waited for Clarissa to transmit the file. "Odin?"

"Yes? Oh, I see. Mister Rosen, I am sending you a file with one of those names on it. You will place your data in that file. When you first open the file, it will ask you to tap six keypads. That will be your password to get to your data files. Whenever the file is opened it will play the game unless you tap those six keypads during the load phase."

"It's a standard encryption method," Jake explained. "Never raises eyebrows. Can't be found unless you know what you're looking for."

Daniel and Clarissa looked down from the viewscreen. Clarissa frowned. "I don't like those sorts of games," she said.

"Well, Daniel does."

"No I don't."

"Don't start with me, you two," Jake warned.

"Oh, all right."

"Fine. I'll get back to you in two or three days. Out."

The image of the Rosens faded and was replaced with the

concert. Jake tapped a keypad to mute the sound. "Odin, their description didn't quite add up," he said. "Run the numbers and see if I'm right."

"Assuming standard space requirements?"

"Everything standard. In fact, take those standards back to the first settlement of Antioch Two."

The bridge was silent for just under two minutes when Odin reported the results of his calculations. "Your estimate appears correct, Jake. There seems to be space unaccounted for in Mister Rosen's statement. That space appears minimal on the first level, substantial on level six. Do you need the actual estimated cubic meters?"

"No, but tell me, could there be enough missing space for a bot repair shop on that first level?"

"A rather large shop, to be factual. Unless other space has been devoted to other uses."

"Such as?"

"A conference room, to state an obvious suggestion."

"Oh, yeah, good point. Okay, so add that room. Enough space for ten to fifteen people to meet in comfort. Is there still enough space left over for a repair shop?"

"Certainly."

"Good. Care to speculate on what's hidden on level six?"

"Not without parameters. I suppose this means I shall have to conduct scans of the world when we arrive?"

"Of course." Jake smiled. "Think of the exercise as a practical test of your ability to scan artificial creations."

"I already passed that test."

"Then you'll just have to pass it again."

Four
Behind the Curtain is Dust

"Sid, why do I have to go along with Evvie on this shoot? Can you give me one good reason?"

Jake was not terribly pleased when Evvie's agent informed him that he had to accompany her to the recording of a promotional infomercial. He believed that he was not a bodyguard, but merely a gloried chauffeur. Getting an explanation was testing his patience, so he came right out and asked Sid directly.

"Okay, fine." Sid's normally ebullient manner was clearly strained. "A friend of Evvie's is planetside. A friend that her mother and I would just as soon not be a friend, if you catch the gist of my hint, Jake."

Oh, swell, Jake thought. *I bet this "friend" is of the male gender, and that her being seen with him wouldn't enhance Evvie's image.*

"Send me a picture of this friend," he said, "and I'll keep my eyes open."

"Done and done. But listen, Jake, it's not that this person is likely to show up at the shoot. The studio there has everything in hand. It's just that, well, y'know, Evvie might tell you she's going somewhere, when actually..."

"Yes, I know." *It's called behaving like a teenager, you twit. Oh, well. Better not endanger this meal ticket.* "Don't worry, Sid. We'll go down, she'll do this shoot, we'll teleport back up, and immediately head for the next stop on the tour."

Sid flashed a thumb up on the screen. "Jake, you the rocket. Later."

Jake smiled to Sid, but as soon as the screen went dark he said, "And you're the asteroid field." He let out an exasperated breath. "Odin, put the ship into auto-control mode. Standard surface drill."

"All systems are functioning at prime levels, so there shouldn't be any problems. If something does occur, I'll contact you."

"As long as it's something you can't handle."

"Of course."

Jake tapped the intercom keypad. "Evvie, it's about time to

37

teleport down."

"'Kay."

"I'll be coming with you this time."

"Oh, Jake..."

"Look, I'm not thrilled, either. But orders are orders."

"Geez, it's not like I'm dating Mac."

I knew it. "Look, either Sid and your mother have your best interests at heart, or they have your image to consider. If I don't follow orders, I could lose this job, or even get sued. So don't complain to me. Be in the teleport room in five minutes."

"Awright."

Jake let out another exasperated breath. "Odin, don't ever agree to let another agent on this ship ever again."

"Only if you promise to follow my guidelines for your personal finances."

Jake let out a strangled cry of frustration.

***

Ten minutes later Jake was watching Evvie get ready to shoot her infomercial. He was somewhat surprised that the process was to start so quickly. He had assumed that time would be spent before getting Evvie into the proper outfit, a professional would apply her makeup, and the director would take everyone through a rehearsal. As it turned out, however, most of these details had been worked out before Skuld had even gotten into orbit. Evvie's lines had been sent to her days ago, along with her outfit and makeup. The whole thing had been worked out with video software in advance. All everyone had to do now was show up and hit their marks.

Jake idly wondered why even that was necessary. An audience could be digitized; the scenes with Evvie and the host could be shot in holorooms; and the whole program stitched together with editing software. An instant later the answer came to him: image. Doing it that way might seem too crafted, and that might undermine how Evvie was being portrayed to the public. She was the nice girl parlaying her talents into a pleasant, inspirational sort of fame. She couldn't be too heavily marketed, because that could undermine her good-girl image.

Think about something else, a voice in his head told Jake, this is starting to give me a headache.

Jake tried to focus on what was going on around him. The

recording of the infomercial had just gotten underway. The theme was not Evvie's music, but instead something called a "Full Teen Beauty System." There weren't just the usual mix of beauty products being shilled, but also a line of clothes, shoes, accessories, and even personal data devices. Apparently, it wasn't enough to look good; there was a whole package to be purchased.

Or as Evvie put in not more than thirty seconds into it, "For the gal who wants to be spiffest of the spiff." Not look, but be.

When he'd first heard that she was doing an infomercial, Jake thought he'd misheard something. The last he knew they had fallen out of favor again. They had become what they had been when the concept was first created, a tool for mediocre products sold by has-beens or never-will-bes. But no, he was assured, the infomercial was back in vogue. At least that's what the market research firm Evvie's distributor had told them. So here she was, doing what not too long ago would have been beyond unhip.

As Evvie and the informercial's host ran through their spiel, Jake looked over the array of products that composed Evvie's "system." He couldn't help but notice right away that everything was colored the brightest hues. Teal, mild lavender, electric orange, and spring green predominated, with pink holding supremacy over the lot. He idly wondered if such shades wouldn't be out of season. Even if it took only a month to put everything together, editing, special effects, and all the rest, the infomercial wouldn't begin running until September. If the production wasn't lucky, it might be November before the spot began airing.

Well, I guess it doesn't really matter, he thought after additional consideration. The colonized areas of some worlds will be in spring, others in summer. Some that would have been in one season will be in a different one, due to planetary orbits and rotation. And on a few worlds "season" is just a calendar thing.

Hold on a sec. If on most worlds the calendar and the seasons don't match up, why stick with it? Convenience? Sure, makes sense. But why keep the local calendar same as Earth standard?

Jake glanced up. Shooting had halted for a moment as Evvie and the host moved from a display counter to talk-show styled chairs. He took out his portacomp and tapped it on. He removed the pen, not wanting to disrupt the crew by speaking his query. He scribbled his question on the screen and waited for an answer. It came in form of an entry in the popular annual publication of odd historical and social miscellany, "Stupid But True."

"Calendar confusion from planet to planet drives most intelligent people crazy," the entry began. *"The Earth-Standard calendar may say it's June, but on the world you happen to land on, it's snowing a up blizzard. The next time this confusion grips you, blame the greeting-card industry for your sad state.*

"When authorities began to allow colonization of worlds beyond Earth, there was discussion of allowing local folks to add or subtract months so that their perception of the time of the year wouldn't be off. However, the greeting-card industry earned vast sums from people sending nice things to each other at certain times of the year, whether an old-fashioned hardcopy card or a multimedia digital file. The industry lobbied hard against any local calendar changes, claiming that subtraction of any month might adversely affect their revenues. They cited the precedent that, when the European powers colonized part of Earth's southern hemisphere, they used their calendar, even though the southern seasons were the reverse of the northern seasons.

"A few anti-corporate activists attempted to counter this lobbying by saying that calendar issues should be decided by local citizens. These activists failed partly because they didn't have economic clout. Mostly, however, they failed because, in attacking this industry, they appeared humorless and unsympathetic. Even normally skeptical commentators mocked the so-called 'card-carrying card-burners' and their crusade.

"So in addition to the smarmy 'Happy Holidays' song files your Aunt Bland always sends, you can add this to your list of reasons to dislike greeting-card corporations."

After digesting this news for a moment, Jake asked himself, *Why am I not surprised?*

He waited calmly as shooting carried on. After he put his perscomp in his pocket, he noticed that similar devices were part of Evvie's system. It wasn't that surprising; after all, if a girl was to be "spiffest of the spiff," she's have plenty of data to manage and files to access and share. What did get his attention was they resembled low-end models that most people tried to avoid buying unless necessary.

Why would that cheap junk be part of this system? he wondered.

Presumably being the spiffest means buying the best brands.

When shooting paused again, Jake's curiosity got the best of him. He wandered over to the display counter. He signaled to one of the producers, who was at his side in a instant.

"A problem, Mister Bonner?"

"No. I was just wondering, why this brand of portables? They aren't a name brand. I thought for sure Evvie would endorse a name like everything else."

The producer gave Jake an expression of bland disinterest. "This was the only manufacturer willing to comply with the standards set for design and shading. The others wanted us to comply with their standards."

"Ah. Thanks."

In other words, he thought, *only this firm was desperate enough to redesign their crap to get Evvie's stamp of approval.*

Jake wandered back to his spot in the corner of the studio to watch the end of the shoot. Up to that point he had questions, but no real surprises. Everything had been either what he'd expected or what, upon reflection, could have been expected. So he was genuinely surprised by the final exchange between the "host" and Evvie.

"Now, Evvie, I'm sure your fans want to know how you chose the products that compose your Full Teen Beauty System."

Evvie managed in the course of her reply to do a fair impression of a young woman imparting important information. "Well, Carol, I'm pleased to tell you, and you out there watching, that everything was brought before me after first undergoing a rigorous selection process." Evvie kept speaking into a camera, even though she was clearly narrating a sequence. "Every product went to a panel of teens, just like you. Nothing went through unspiff adults. These teens rated everything for looks, ease of use, price, and for how they fit into my system. Finally, I tried everything out myself. After all, I couldn't put by name on anything that I didn't like."

"Sounds like a lot of work, Evvie." The host managed to do a good impression of someone interested and surprised with what her guest was saying. It was, of course, an act; her statement was merely the signal to end a narrated sequence.

"It was. But we did it that way so my fans can believe in this system. It wasn't created on the spur of the moment. Nothing was

41

thrown together."

"Y'know, the old saying is, 'A system is only as good as the parts that make up that system.'"

"That's a straight jump, Carol. My system works, 'cause everything works."

"Well, your fans don't just have to take your word for it." The host turned to face her camera. "We previewed Evvie's Full Teen Beauty System to some very excited fans. Let's see if they liked it as much as Evvie does."

Jake shook his head as the director paused the shoot to prepare for the final scene of the infomercial. If he hadn't heard it himself, he never would have believed it.

Oh, brother, he mused. *Not only did they send this system to focus group, but they're actually proud of that fact. They actually believe that this lack of spontaneity and big marketing push is a selling point. Random chance and original thought are to be avoided at all costs.*

But are you surprised? Look at how much creds are riding on all this. How many people, how many companies, have something at stake.

Including me, now that I think about it.

And I can't blame Evvie for this. She's just going along with the script she's been handed. It's an old one, too. Goes back over a century and a half, as a matter of fact.

Now that I think about that, it probably goes back even farther. The Beatles didn't get where they did without selling themselves pretty heavily early on. Sinatra and Elvis made movies and specials to keep their careers going. The classical composers had to keep audiences or patrons pleased every now and again to survive. Hell, Shakespeare's plays have elements in them to keep the proles in the pits from throwing food at the actors. Evvie's just following a long and well-established tradition of artists with market savvy doing what they can earn a living.

Doesn't mean her music's in that class, though. At least that's something.

***

The following evening Evvie was once again on stage as part of her tour. While keeping modest attention to the show, Jake got back in contact with his other employers. He wanted to know if the

Rosens had obtained the information he'd requested, and wanted more details on Antioch Two.

After getting them on the screen and exchanging greetings, Jake saw Daniel tap a few keypad on his end. "I'm highlighting the file with all the data we collected on the guardbots," Daniel said.

"Odin?"

"Copying the file, Jake," Odin replied. "Allow me some time to examine the data."

"Sure." Jake turned back to the Rosens. "Did you find out anything else about those bots?"

"We discovered that different bots are put on different patrols in different places each day," Daniel said. "We weren't able to find out if there's a schedule of some sort."

"Don't worry about that now. There'll be plenty of time to figure that out later. By the way, how did you uncover that fact, anyway?"

Daniel looked mildly embarrassed. "Clarissa and I would pause behind them and check their unit numbers."

"Okay. At least you didn't break any rules. That's good."

"I have analyzed the data, Jake," Odin interrupted.

"Anything of importance?"

"The guard robots deployed are all eight years old. They appear to have been purchased in bulk."

"Trade-in, or new purchase?"

"That isn't in the file. I will attempt to ascertain that at a future date, if it's important."

"Probably not, but it might be useful. Anything else?"

"These robots are armed with stunners and entangling restraints. They are controlled via data signals sent over the air on wireless frequencies. The only internal controls on these models are navigational, as well as a protocol to defend themselves if attacked. The robots were built to transmit audio and video data."

"Yet the Rosens peeked at them, and nothing happened," Jake pointed out.

"True. A logical conclusion would be that the robots were not so equipped."

Jake turned back to the Rosens again. "Have you ever seen the bots transmit signals? Are they used to monitor your people, or do they just stand there?"

"They stand, or they move around," Clarissa said. "I've never seen one pointed at someone."

"Neither have I," Daniel added.

"Odin, that is something worth following up on."

"I concur, and shall do so."

"Now, Daniel, Clarissa, I'd like some information on your lives."

"Our lives?" Clarissa asked. Her open face closed a window or two. "Isn't that a bit personal?"

"Not your lives. The lives of your people. What you do during the day, during the week. That sort of thing."

"Oh."

"For example, how do people start the work day?"

"Well, the first awake are the executives, the foremen, day-shift dome crews, and the teachers. They gather in the cafeteria for first breakfast at six. Then at seven all the other workers eat."

"Then what?"

"Then everyone goes to work."

"Hoverbuses transport workers and foremen to the mines," Daniel added. "Workers at the other domes take hovercars."

"And everyone works on site until when?" Jake asked.

"First-shift lunch is in the cafeteria at eleven-thirty," Clarissa answered, "and everyone else eats an hour later."

"Everyone has to eat in the cafeteria? There's no onsite meals?"

"No."

"That is not a very efficient use of time," Odin observed.

"I don't think efficiency has anything to do with it," Jake said. "It does keep the bulk of the workforce together throughout the day. That would make the workers much easier to monitor."

"I suppose there is a certain logic to that scheme, but it is flawed."

"And that's a surprise, why?"

When Odin didn't reply, Jake returned to the Rosens. "I take it this is the way things have always been done."

"Always," Clarissa said.

"Okay. So I take it at the end of the work day the same thing happens. There's a first-shift of dinner, followed by the main dinner."

"Well, the executives and their families eat dinner in the reception room on level one, but otherwise that's right."

"And after dinner everyone goes back to their quarters, does whatever, goes to sleep, and the next day the cycle starts all over again."

"Six days a week," Clarissa said, a slight stridency in her voice.

"Let me guess. Sunday is everyone's day off."

"Yes."

"So what happens on Sundays?"

"That's the only day that we can eat in our quarters. We can take part in home activities, hobbies, attend a monthly cultural club meeting. There are school programs in the afternoon, and a dance in the cafeteria in the evening."

"Don't forget Maxis' awards," Daniel said.

"At one in the afternoon Maxis holds a ceremony to announce the worker of the week. The winner gets the next day off, a certificate, and a chance to win 'worker of the year.'"

"And what's that prize worth?" Jake asked.

"A week's vacation off-world with one of the executives and their family."

"Lame, but I suppose it could be worse."

"How?"

"Only giving a trip to the worker of the decade. Or no trip, just a week off work. Trust me, there are lots of crappy prizes in the universe." Jake glanced at the small screen showing Evvie's concert. Her routine suggested she was just past the halfway mark. "Okay, well, that's going to help. Now, there's something that's been bothering me. I don't know if you have the answer, but I'll ask anyway. How is it that off-worlders don't know about what's going on? I mean, presumably all that gold and silver are shipped off Antioch Two. How is it that whoever's picking the stuff up doesn't see what's going on?"

"I can answer that," Daniel said. "My father works in the processing plant."

"Great. Enlighten me."

"The raw ore comes out of the mines and is put on a conveyor to a maglev train to be run into the plant. The plant turns the raw ore into pure minerals and placed into storage units. The units are sent to the transport pad, where the cargo ships pick them up. All the contacts between the ships and the ground are through signals."

"And there's never any face time between the shippers and, say, the executives? It's all audio, video, or data?"

"Yes."

"Odin, want to analyze this?"

"The system would seem to be effective in preventing locals or off-worlders from stealing any pieces of mineral. The operation on Antioch Two is fairly standard. I must confess that I am surprised that no shipper would inspect the plant or the storage units."

"If they opened the units at their destination and didn't find gold, or silver, or whatever," Jake said, "they'd notice, and start flaming everyone." Jake frowned for an instant to think. "It almost sounds like this is an off-book arrangement."

"You could be correct."

"'Off-book,' Jake?" Daniel asked. "What does that mean?"

"It means that whoever is picking up your minerals is doing something they're not supposed to. That's something else we'll look into down the road. One last question, and I'll let you go. I assume that you there aren't worked till you die."

"No. When a couple reaches retirement age, they get a reception on a Sunday, and then they're gone."

"Gone?"

"Gone. Sent off-world, I guess."

"What if the husband is a few years older than his wife?"

"Doesn't happen, at least not to most of us."

"You see," Clarissa said, "no one is allowed to have children without permission from the top. Permission tends to be granted in groups. Three couples one month, four the next, three after that. Workers are only allowed two children, unless one gets conceived on one of those 'worker of the year' trips. All the workers are around the same age, give or take five years."

"There is a steady population," Odin remarked. "Therefore, it would be a simple task to plan for the population's needs. Variables are reduced, leading to efficiencies in supply ordering and overall planning."

"But not exactly a free population," Jake commented.

"No."

"Now do you see why we're so unhappy?" Clarissa asked.

"I can sympathize," Jake told her, "but there might be more reasons to overthrow Maxis than the mere ideal of liberty."

"Mere?"

"There is a bigger picture here, Clarissa. Give us some time to do some digging. Until our next conversation, keep your eyes open and your mouths shut. I won't be able to help you for a couple months yet. Don't get into trouble before then."

"We won't."

"Good. I'll try to get back to you next week."

"Thank you."

"Sure." The screen went dark. "Odin, I think you should chase down this retirement question first. Let's find out what happens when you get too old to work for Maxis."

"Very well. Any reason why that should be a priority?"

"I want to know well ahead of time if I'm going to have run through the dome screaming, 'Soylent Green is made from people!'"

"I assume to perfect your less-than-stellar impression. By the way, Jake, I believe that Evvie's concert is just about over."

"Just in time."

Five
Secrets To Spare

Jake walked to the teleport room, still thinking about Antioch Two. Suddenly he caught himself. Why was he going to the teleport to meet Evvie? There didn't seem to be any real reason to do so. It wasn't like they were pals, and they'd talk about their days. Evvie certainly couldn't get lost from there to her room. The only explanation that he could come up with was that it was his job to look after her for the duration of the tour. If this meant meeting her when she teleported up, so be it.

He walked into the room and down behind the teleport control console. He tapped a few keypads then said, "Evvie, ready to teleport?"

"Uh, hold it a bit." Several seconds passed. "Okay, I'm ready."

"Teleporting, now."

Jake tapped the main control. One of the three teleport pads began to glow green. A ghostly green light appeared over it for two seconds. But when the glowing stopped, there was no Evvie. Lying on the pad was her teleport bracelet.

"Oh, for God's sake." Jake sighed. "Odin, Evvie took off her bracelet. Can you lock in on her?"

"Her last position had her with several other humans."

"Stand by to teleport me down."

"I do not think that would be wise, Jake."

"Why?"

"My sensors tell me that she's just stepped into a hovercar with several others."

"Oh, this is terrific. If we don't find her and get her back, we could be in a lot of trouble. Home in on that vehicle. See where it goes."

"I shall try."

Jake waited at the console. *Now she's gone and done it. This is exactly the "unauthorized access" I agreed to prevent her from getting involved with. I she trying to get me in trouble? Is she trying to get me fired? Or is she just too dumb to know what kind of a fix this puts me in?*

Has to be the last. She's not smart enough to plan something like this out.

Wait a sec. "Odin, find out if she's still carrying her messager."

"I believe so. Yes, she is. Shall I contact her? I should say that such a signal probably won't be ideal for teleport."

"It's not that. I've got an idea about how to get that bracelet back on her, and her back on this ship. Let me know where she stops."

***

Evvie never really liked the sound her Perc personal communicator made when a message came in. She tried to program in better sounds, like one of her hits, or the theme to *Captain Sandy*. Unfortunately her efforts resulted in her managing to turn the alert chime into a loud and thoroughly uncool whine. But she was able to switch from alert sound to silent vibration. Actually, the motion was fun. It almost always got attention, and occasionally even felt good.

She hadn't been expecting a call while she was out. Jake couldn't find her, not without that bracelet, which of course went with nothing. Sensors couldn't pick her out of the crowd at the club, and she was dancing too much.

"Hey, your Perc," one of her friends said, "it's dancing!"

"Lemme check it."

Evvie took it out of her blouse pocket. She tapped a key, and the tiny screen lit up. "Relay message, audio, from your mother," the screen read. "Accept or decline?"

"It's Mom," she told her friends.

"You better take it."

"It's a voice call."

"Ew." The other girl pointed away from the dance floor to a pair of doors. "Take it in there."

"Oh, spiff!" Evvie knew the bathrooms wouldn't entirely drown out the noise of the club. But it would muffle it enough to make it seem like she was just listening to loud music.

She began to drag her friends along, then stopped. "Oh, wait! If Mom hears you guys, I'm busted for sure."

"We'll stay out here."

"Watch the door for me."

"Sure!"

Evvie jogged to the women's bathroom. Once inside she looked

49

around to make certain no one else was inside. Luckily no one was. She relaxed. Her friends would keep other girls out. Now she could take the call without worrying about her mother finding out. She pressed "Accept" on the screen and prepared to explain why she hadn't been able to talk immediately.

A second later the air behind her glowed green. She turned just in time to see Jake materialize in the room. She was almost certain the smile on his face had appeared before the rest of him did.

"What are you doing here?"

"Bringing you back." He snapped a teleport bracelet onto her right wrist and tapped a red button on it. "Odin, now." A moment later they were aboard Jake's ship. An instant after that Jake took the bracelet off her wrist.

"Hey, I was having fun!"

"Unauthorized fun," he replied.

"So?"

"So? So I signed a contract that prevents me from allowing you to have any contact that your mother and your agent don't approve of. If they didn't okay your clubbing, I have no choice but to bring you back here."

"They don't want me to club with my friends."

"Take it up with them."

"Oh yeah? Well, maybe I will."

Jake smiled again. "Oh, please do so."

"Huh?"

"Go ahead and tell them what happened. If they don't find out from checking the local news. Either way, I can say that I had no idea you would do this. But I do have a way to prevent it from happening again."

Jake pulled a tiny wafer from his shirt pocket and held it in front of her face. "Know what this is?"

Something in Evvie told her to be more suspicious and less stubborn. "No. What is it?"

"It's a subcutaneous tracker."

"What's that?"

"An implant locator chip."

Evvie sucked in a breath. "Implant?"

One of her earliest memories, and the first time she felt real fear, was when she was a preschooler and had to go to a dentist. One of her baby teeth had not come in properly, and her parents took her to the dentist for oral surgery. Up to that day she had never seen anything so terrifying as the instruments the dentist had arrayed next to her for the surgery. And if that wasn't enough, she remembered waking up during the operation and seeing a masked man sticking something into her mouth.

Ever since that day Evvie had a deep and abiding fear of anything artificial being put into her body. She zealously cared for her teeth after someone mentioned that if a cavity got too big a filling would be put in. She insisted on strong anesthesia whenever she was operated on, which fortunately had only occurred once so far. As a young teenager and aspiring star, she prayed night and day for a decent cup size to avoid breast implants. She was even more thankful that piercings had gone out of style before she'd started on her music career.

So it was with a great deal of trepidation that she looked at the chip Jake held in front of her. "You'd stick that, into me?"

"If I can't trust you no to pull another stunt like this." He seemed oblivious to her horror. "So promise me that you'll confess to your mother and Sid, and let me off the hook."

"And you won't let anyone stick that thing in me?"

"No."

"It's a deal." Still angry, but too concerned to continue the fight, Evvie took off the bracelet. "I'm tired. I'm going to bed. I'll make those calls in the morning." She elbowed past him and walked directly to her room.

It took her longer than usual to get to sleep that night.

***

A week later Evvie was again out and about, this time on a date with a popular young actor. But unlike her previous foray, the date was authorized by her mother and her agent. The night had been arranged, a schedule was in place, and nothing bad was to happen to the music star.

Which was why Evvie asked Jake for his help this time around. "Could you help me bail part-way through?"

"Why? It's not like you've been on lots of dates so far. And I take this guy has quite a bit going for him; handsome, rich, popular,... young."

She shook her head. "Don't you follow the news?"

51

"Yes."

She rolled her eyes. "Yeah, right. If you did, you'd know that Mark is a complete doze. He's totally bought into the 'play nice' act. He takes his dates to blah restaurants, never goes to clubs, listens to music from the last century."

"And plans to abstain from sex until marriage." Jake folded his arms across his chest. "Why, Evvie, I didn't know you were such a bad girl at heart."

She glanced at the floor. "That has nothing to do with it."

"I'm not entirely convinced, for some strange reason."

She looked up at him. "Jake, please, you gotta help me out, this one time. Mark is so L-7 it's almost unhuman."

"No, and the word is 'inhuman.'"

She frowned for a moment. "You're always complaining about me being shallow, right? Well, I've heard that Mark is even more shallow than me."

"And who told you this?"

"A famous young actress who went out with him a few times. She told me all he ever wanted to talk about was his latest job, and the last personal growth book he read."

"And this opinion comes from an actress? What, she wasn't happy he was talking about her?"

"Well, yeah. I mean, he's an actor, and he didn't have a clue as to what she was in at the time. And that every third sentence of his was some self-help expression. And that every time she tried to bring up something current, he'd ignore her and go back to whatever he was talking about." She pointed to him. "You shouldn't want me to go out with him. I mean, if I'm shallow, he's... he's..."

"Almost nonexistent?"

"Yes! That's it! He barely exists."

Jake sighed. "All right. There will no sneaking off, promise?"

"I promise. All I want you to do is pull me out when I call you."

"I'm not going to teleport you out of a restaurant, or any other crowded place. At least not without any warning. It's bad manners."

"Don't worry. After we eat, I'll pretend like I'm sick. I'll go away and call you. I'll go back, tell him I'm feeling bad, and call it a night. You beam me up, and that's that."

He looked at her for a moment. "If I get flagged on this play, you're going to take the blame, Evvie."

"Nothing's going to happen. Mom never bugs me about stomach aches."

"What do I get in return?"

"I'll... I'll think of something. Something nice. I promise I'll do something for you, or get you something. Please?"

Jake sighed. "Okay. But this is the only time you ask me for a favor like this, Evvie. Understood?"

"Got it. Thanks!" Evvie dashed back to her room to get ready for the date.

***

Jake had been reluctant to agree to her suggestion. He wanted to use the opportunity to get back in touch with the Rosens. The conversations didn't go on for all that long, but this time he had some information for them. It was complicated, and might take some time to explain.

Oh, well, he thought, *I'll just have to call as soon as Evvie leaves*.

Unfortunately his idea went awry. The Rosens didn't respond to his first attempt to contact them, nor to other attempts made every fifteen minutes. Finally, after an hour of trying, he was able to get through to them. His first question was why it had taken so long for them to respond.

"We only just got in," Daniel said. He appeared winded.

"What's happened?"

"One of the mine conveyors broke down. Lots of people were called in to help move minerals, or fix the conveyor."

"Anyone hurt?"

"No, everyone's fine. But it looks like we're going to have to have a new conveyor shipped in pretty soon."

"Okay. Well, I don't have much time, so pay attention. You remember last time we talked about what happens to your people when they retire? Well, Odin and I did some digging and calling around. It seems that your retirees are sent off-world, specifically to the 'Shady Glade' complex on Magnolia."

"What's this complex?" Clarissa asked.

"The accepted term is 'golden years living center.' A retirement community, basically."

"So why not tell us that?"

Jake smiled. "This is part where you have to pay attention. Now,

Robert Collins

interstellar law requires employers to set aside part of an employee's income for a retirement plan. It's called a 'pension,' if you've never heard of the concept. Furthermore, employers are forbidden to maintain contracts with other employers that don't adhere to interstellar pension law."

"That second part doesn't make sense."

"Sorry. What I meant was 'corporate employers.' A large corporation can make contracts with a smaller firm that, for one reason or another, can't set up some sort of retirement plans. But if a business has the resources, isn't a temporary colonial employer, or has some other exemption, it has to set up these pension plans."

"And Maxis hasn't set up any for us?"

"No. If that was true, one, you'd all work till you die. Two, he couldn't sell minerals on the open market or contract with shippers to get off your planet."

"So what's the problem, Jake?" Daniel asked.

"I'm getting there. Now, not everyone can save enough for retirement. Some people never get to save anything. This has been true for a couple of centuries. As a result, governments set up assistance programs so that retirees don't end up starving to death, or dying from preventable diseases, or anything else that might keep them from living a normal life.

"Now, Maxis is supposed to pay for your retirement. But he ships people to Magnolia, lists the creds set aside as 'severance,' and pays them into accounts in the workers' names on Magnolia. Shady Glade gets the retirees, tells the authorities that they don't have any retirement plans, so the government sends the creds into those accounts in the workers' names."

"And who gets those creds?"

"Maxis and the owners of Shady Glade split the income. You see, your people never retire; they get fired, as least as far as the files are concerned. Shady Glade isn't getting retirees with pension plans; they're getting indigents with not a credit to their names."

"So how do these people live once they get there?"

"Fine. Everything's provided for, medical care, food, recreation, even calls back home to the relatives."

"How does this Shady Glade pay for that?"

"Apparently, residents of Shady Glade live incredibly long lives."

54

"Really?"

Jake sighed. "Unrealistically long lives, Daniel. In at least one case we found, years after a death certificate was logged with the local coroner's office."

"Oh. I see."

"Right. Maxis and Shady Glade's owners are making a nice little profit on their deal. This, combined with a few other bits of data, are making me wonder how many other accounts are being padded."

Daniel suddenly sat a little straighter and his eyes widened. Jake guessed that an idea had just come to him. "Now that we know this, can't we just call in the Earth government to help us?"

"A nice thought," Jake said with total sincerity. *Good of you to start using your brain*, he thought with much less sincerity. "One problem with that." *Two if you count my loss of potential income.* "A government investigation is going to take time. Subjects would have to advised of their rights. Disclosures could be leaked. It's possible that as soon as something gets going, Maxis and anyone else involved off your world will disappear before any arrests can be made. Maybe that puts you in charge, but more likely its puts someone else in who will run your planet like Maxis does now, except that the replacement won't be tied to all these schemes."

"We might still need your help," Daniel said, "but if Maxis' successor isn't as tarnished, ousting him will be even more difficult."

"Precisely. So, just be patient. Odin and I will continue our data mining. "

"Jake, there are some areas of the dome that we don't know what goes on in," Clarissa said. "Should we try to find out...?"

"No," Jake snapped. "Don't take any silly risks! We can find out much easier than you can without any real risk."

"Jake," Odin said.

"Not now. Look, this revolution doesn't start until I say so."

"Jake,..."

"I said not now. You two go taking risks like that, and this thing ends before it begins. And you get picked up, there's nothing I can do to save you."

"Evvie's calling."

Jake gasped. "Oh, shit!" He raised a hand to the Rosens. "Look, I gotta go. Just sit tight, alright? Sit tight and be patient. Out."

Jake glanced down the corridor. "Dammit! I'd better meet her in person."

"Should I teleport her up?"

"Not till I get there, and can catch my breath!"

He leapt up from his seat and dashed to the teleport room. He sat down behind the console, took a few breaths to calm himself, then said, "Okay, Odin. Bring her up."

Evvie materialized a minute later. An instant after she appeared she put her hands on her hips. Her face was a mask of rage. "What took you so long? I thought I'd never get away."

"Look, I'm terribly sorry. I...I just got a little busy. When Odin tried to let me know you were calling, I shrugged him off. I'm sorry, okay?"

"Well, okay. I'm spending the rest of the night in my room."

"Sure. Fine. Good night." He smiled to her. He waved behind her as she left the teleport room. Once she was gone he let out a long, silent breath.

Whew, that was close, he thought. *I've got to be more careful. I don't think she or Sid would appreciate me working another job on the side.*

Well, this minor crisis is over. Move on, and in one more month it's no longer an issue.

***

When she went to bed Evvie was cross. She was still cross when she woke up the next morning. Her black mood dogged her through breakfast, her shower, her choosing of the day's style, the actual dressing process, and her putting on her makeup. Just as she was about to step out of her room, a thought entered her mind.

Why was Jake so sorry last night? she wondered.

She had gotten into the habit of her taking his unspiff remarks and highbrow insults in stride. Either Jake would say something and she'd reply, or he's say something and she'd ignore him. Last night he not only said he was sorry for being late, but he actually sounded like he meant it. He had never said anything nice or compassionate to her that seemed to be an honest reflection of his feelings; he was either being nasty or polite.

Which led her to ask the next question: *Why?*

Obviously, she decided, *he was doing something that held his attention. But what could it be?*

It couldn't be a relationship. There was no reason for him to keep that a secret, and it wasn't like she'd be jealous of him or anything. It probably wasn't another job. What else could he be doing that would take him away from this one?

I know! He's spying on me. He's telling some scuzzy netzine all about me.

Wait. What have I done since he's been escorting me that they'd care about? Well, my sneaking off, but he had me come clean on that to Sid and Mom. Why would he tell anyone else about it? And last night? Well, it's not like that was any big secret. Except for me jumping early, and that's no big thing.

Well, he must be up to something, and I want to know what that is.

She left her room and stomped up the control area. Unfortunately Jake was no where to be seen. *I'll bet the computer knows where he is. So how do I get ahold of it? Wait, you just say it's name. Which is... which is...*

"Uh, Odin?"

"Yes, Miss Martini?"

"Where's Jake? I need to talk to him."

"Jake is presently carrying out a series of routine maintenance checks on the sub-light engines. Unless what you have to say is of a dire nature, I suggest you wait until he's finished."

"It's sort of dire. I want to know why he was late picking me up last night."

"Miss Martini, that is not a dire question. I recall Jake giving you an answer when you returned."

"No, he just said he was busy. He didn't say what he was busy doing."

"If that was not to your satisfaction, you should take it up with him."

"Why don't you tell me?"

"I am not authorized to answer that question."

"Well, how do you get authorized?"

"Jake instructs me to tell you."

Evvie let out a strangled cry. "This is a black hole! Won't anyone tell me what's going on around here?" If she had been paying close attention, she might have heard the slightest hint of an exasperated sigh coming from the speaker system. As it was, she was involved in her own feeling of frustration.

"I am sorry that you are upset, Miss Martini," Odin said slowly. "But, and please do not take this the wrong way, that is not my concern. If Jake wishes to tell you what goes on in his life outside of working for you, that is his prerogative. If you are unhappy with the situation, discuss it with him."

"You two are keeping something from me, I know it!"

"What's going on here?" Jake asked. He walked in carrying small device.

Evvie turned to face him. She pressed her face into the angriest expression she could. "You're up to something!" Part of her wanted to continue demanding answers. But so far she hadn't been too successful. She decided that since she hadn't gotten anywhere, she'd have to try a new tactic.

"Jake, I want to know why you were late picking me up."

"Why?"

"Because I deserve to know."

"No, you don't."

"Yes, I do."

"Evvie, please,..."

"Aha! There! You're being nice to me. You're definitely up to something."

"It's nothing to do with you."

"How do I know that?"

Jake opened his mouth to speak, but hesitated. He closed his mouth, glared at her, then sighed. "Look. I'm not spying on you. I'm not recording you in the shower. I'm not sending your lyrics or dance routines to other pop stars. What I do on my time is my business."

"Oh, really? Suppose I tell Sid, huh?"

"Tell him what? That I was late helping you get out of a date that he and your mother arranged for you?"

Evvie felt her strength wane, but only for a moment. "Tell me, Jake! Tell me, or... or... or I'll get Sid to look into it. And I'll insist he hire a new pilot! And I'll have the creds we've paid you retracted from your account!"

That clearly plunged deep into Jake's heart. He appeared to consider various forms of getting back at her, which probably included violence, embarrassment, blackmail, and more violence. Fortunately, the rage within him boiled briefly. He pointed to the couch in an obvious gesture of surrender. She sat down first. He sat down next to her, some space between them.

"Right before Sid hired me," he explained, "a couple contacted me from Antioch Two. They want me to help them overthrow their planet's dictator."

"So why should you care?"

"Because the planet mines gold, silver, and other precious metals," Odin said without prompting. "They are offering Jake five percent of their profits, every year, for the rest of his life, if he assists them in their revolution."

"So what does all that have to do with me?"

"Nothing," Jake said.

"Even though Antioch Two is one of the last stops on your tour," added Odin.

"You're not going to attack while I'm doing my show, are you?" Evvie was horrified at the brief thought of one of her shows being disrupted by civil unrest. She didn't quite notice the dirty look Jake gave to the ceiling.

"Of course not," Jake answered, his face a mask of reassurance. "We will be checking their defenses and such during your performance, but that's it. I don't plan to return until after you are safely off my ship. Happy?"

Evvie crossed her arms over her chest. She was quiet for a moment, then she said, "You should have told me sooner."

"No, I shouldn't have. Now do you see that this wasn't something that you needed to know?"

"Well, still..."

Jake pointed at her. "Don't tell anyone. This is a delicate job. Any leaks about this could put people's lives in danger. Not the least of which, I might add, is your own. You're the one who will be going down to perform, not me."

"Okay, okay. I won't tell a soul. Thank you for being so honest with me." She smiled as pleasantly as she could. She stood up and walked to the holoroom to rehearse for her next show.

***

That night as she was getting ready to go to sleep, Evvie found herself wondering if she ought to keep her promise to Jake. She was surprised at this bit of reflection. To her, either a promise meant something and she kept it, or it didn't and she didn't. She also wasn't the sort of person to think too much about a decision; almost always one choice or the other worked for her. But there she was, in her room, changing from her day clothes into her pajamas, asking herself if she should keep Jake's secret or let it out.

Telling Sid and Mom would be a mean thing to do, she thought. *Jake isn't blessed with my talent, or the creds I've earned from my talent. He's trying to make a living. It would be wrong of me to... to hurt his income like that.*

Still, it would be a way to get back at him for all the things he's done to me, like dis my music and be late getting me out from the paws of that actor-geek. Yeah, but that still wouldn't be nice of me. And he could tell lots of people about how mean I was to him, and that wouldn't do me any good.

Well, maybe I don't have to be the meanie. I could tell Sid and Mom, let them figure out if this is a problem, and if it is they'll do... whatever. No, wait, I'd still be telling them, and Jake could still blame me.

Okay, so maybe we could make it his fault. How would it be his fault?

Well, revolutions involve fighting, right? Yeah, and usually it's either fighting bad people, or bad people doing the fighting. So, maybe he's put me in some kind of danger, and that would be his fault.

Except that he hasn't actually gotten me involved in his little side job. If I don't tell Sid and Mom, I'm probably never going to be in danger. He'll finish jumping me around, and that's that. In fact, if I stay out of it, I'll not only keep myself safe, but maybe keep those people on that planet safe as well.

What happened next to Evvie's train of thought rarely occurred to her outside of her home studio and rehearsal space. She had an honest-to-Heaven, sure as death and taxes, 110-percent bolt of pure inspiration.

Would it be right for me to completely stay out? she asked herself.

I do have some pretty spiff bank accounts. I could buy supplies and stuff for them. I mean, wouldn't that be pretty cool of me? Wouldn't that boost my rep awfully high?

Wait. Why should I stop there? What if I got more involved than just giving my creds? I could ask Jake to let me take some part in this revolution thing.

I wonder if any other celeb has done anything like this?

Evvie's first impulse was to call for the computer to ask him that question. She prevented herself from asking it out loud when she realized that the computer was smart enough to answer. For if he was indeed that intelligent, he might be intelligent enough to figure out why she was asking. And if he could figure that out, he could very well tell Jake, and he would probably try to talk her out of her idea before she's had a chance to decide about it.

But not asking the computer meant having to do research. That was one of the few parts of school that was difficult for Evvie, along with science and short lunches. Her idea was so important to her that she plunged in anyway. She searched through the ship's considerable database to find out if any celebrity had ever taken part in a revolution.

At first she was disappointed to learn that many had. However, as she read deeper into each story, she found that the "revolution" in question was almost always a social one, not an actual struggle to overthrow a real dictator. Quite a few had lent their support to revolutions, donating time, giving their money, or taking part in protests outside the regime in question. But to her surprise, Evvie discovered that as yet no famous person had actually played an active role in an effort to oust an evil ruler.

She gasped. "I would be the first," she muttered aloud.

She came back to realty an instant later. *Well*, she mused, *I couldn't actually risk my life. That would be stupid. But there ought to be some real things for me to do short of putting myself in danger that I can do to help out. Of course, I'm not quite sure what those things would be, but I'm sure Jake would know.*

But if I did really do something to help this revolution,...

For one thing, my rep would really leap. How could anyone say I wasn't a nice girl then? Hey, I helped bring freedom to a planet. That's the ultimate good girl deed. And those critics? Heck, they couldn't even touch me. I'm a freedom fighter, what are you? Hey, even Jake would have to stop making fun of me and my music.

And that's not the only spiff thing about it. I mean, I would be the first, after all. Every other celeb before me would be nothing compared to me. Madonna, Britney, Tamilya, they'd all come in a distant second to Evvie. Heck, maybe I could drop my last name and be one of those one-name stars.

This would make me the pop star I've always dreamed about being.

Okay, head out of the sky, girl. First, I've got to get Jake, Sid, and Mom behind me on this. So who do I try for first?

Well, I could probably convince Sid pretty easily. Once he sees the benefits to my fame and everything, he'd go along. And once he's behind me, he'll help me talk Mom into getting on board. And as long as I'm not going to be in any real danger, she shouldn't have any problem with this.

Which leaves Jake.

Well, he should be happy to get some help. I mean, sure, he's a smart guy, but he's got to need some help with this. And if he isn't,... Well, wait, there are plenty of media rights to this. There's the drama rights, memoir rights, licensing. I think I'd keep the music rights for myself. But everything else we could share, or let him have the bigger stake, or even let him control if he wants to. I bet once I get on this, his income from this will double or even triple.

So, everyone wins in this deal. The people on that planet get free, Jake gets rich, and I become the undisputed Queen of Pop.

This is going to be beyond spiff!

Six
For Freedom & Big Sales Figures

"We have now achieved orbit over Antioch Two."

"Thank you, Odin." Jake turned to Sid and Evvie, sitting across from him on the couch. He was surprised that the two wanted to talk to him, but also profoundly suspicious. Here they were, over the planet that just a week ago Evvie found out he was going to liberate once he'd left her employment. What would have made this truly worrisome would be if Evvie's mother was there as well. Apparently she was busy with an interview that she couldn't avoid. Her absence didn't ease Jake's concerns one millimeter.

"What did you two want to talk to me about?" he asked. He tried not to sound like he was giving anything away.

"Well, Jakie, "Sid said, "Evvie's told me about what you're planning to do here after the tour."

"She what?"

Sid raised his hands quickly. "Don't sweat it, buddy! We're not here to rain on your parade or anything. Matter of fact, I'm pleased as the winner of the galactic lottery that you're helping those colonists down there!"

Jake was stunned for an instant. "You are?"

"Absolutely. Awfully decent of you, dude. It's just too darn bad that everyone doesn't share you concern for the welfare of others."

"Thanks." *I have a bad feeling about this*, Jake thought.

Sid smiled. "Jake, Evvie's got something she wants to ask you."

Evvie sat up straight. "Jake, would you be willing to let me help you in this revolution thing?"

Jake's jaw moved, but he couldn't even manage to get a squeak out. Thoughts, questions, and finally replies raced around his brain. Words were inadequate to the task. At long last, all Jake could say was, "Why?"

"Tell him, Sid."

"Right, kiddo." Sid rose. "Think of it, Jake." His arms began to flutter. "In the whole history of music, in the whole history of human culture, there's been many celebs willing to give creds to a cause.

Speak for a cause. Even get arrested for a cause. But never has there been a star willing to risk their life and fight for a cause!

"Think of it: Evvie will actually take part in a revolution. She will make a stand for freedom that will... will be bigger than any stand taken by any celebrity in the whole span of recorded time!

"Of course, the actual danger to Evvie will have to be minimized as much as possible. She wants to help this revolution, but not become a martyr or anything. But I'm sure you can figure out ways for her take an active role without putting her life at extreme risk, Jake. You're a smart man.

"If you're still not certain, well, think of all those great men and women who have fought for freedom. George Washington. Winston Churchill. Lech Walesa. Vaclav Havel. I could go on for hours. Now, think about this. To their exalted ranks, you will be able to add two new names: Jake Bonner and Evangelyne Martini.

"And we mean that, Jake. We are prepared to grant you five percent of the gross profits of music rights, maybe as much as ten. We will allow you to name your share of the drama and licensing rights. The memoir rights to your story will be exclusively yours. And that's on top of what the people planetside are paying you, don't forget."

Evvie's eyes met Jake's. "So, Jake, will you sign me up?"

Jake stared off into the distance. "I think I am going to be sick." He sighed. "I'm going to regret this, but fine. You want in, you're in. But I give the orders, right?"

"Yeah, sure. Whatever you say."

As he shook Sid and Evvie's hands, all Jake could think was, *What have I gotten myself into now?*

***

As he prepared to teleport down to Antioch Two, Jake surprised himself by being happy that Maxis was a fan of Evvie's. Normally planetary leaders didn't attend pop concerts. Security concerns were the usual reason given, but more often than not they were simply too busy to bother. If they did show up, it was because the concert was something very special, such as the first of a tour, or a major band reunion, or something else. Maxis could have had reasons not to attend Evvie's show, but he was there along with everyone else on the planet.

That meant that security would be there, too. They would not be close to Maxis' quarters, and therefore close to the executive meeting room and the executive lavatory. Jake would be able to bug both places without the danger of an uncomfortable encounter with a guard.

Jake stepped onto the teleport platform. "Ready, Odin?"

"One moment."

Jake waited.

"All monitoring devices are now being spoofed, Jake. But be careful not to make any normal-volume noises or move anything."

"Of course. Teleport."

He materialized in the executive meeting room. It was not completely dark; two light-threads illuminated two old-fashioned paintings at one end of the room. Name plates under each identified the one on the right as Maxis' father and the one on the left as his grandfather. They framed a chair at one end of the meeting room table that was taller and clearly cushier than the others around the table. Jake instantly knew that the chair belonged to Maxis.

He walked up to it slowly and stopped next to it. He took his perscomp out of a chest pocket in his dark jumpsuit. He aimed the device at a spot on the table in front of the chair and a few centimeters from edge. He tapped the screen a few times, waited, shifted the perscomp to his left hand, and opened his right hand. A minute later a chunk of the interior of the table materialized above his palm.

Almost everyone who had one soon discovered that a useful but less-than-obvious application of the teleport was in the planting of listening devices. If someone on the ground could direct a sensor onto an exact location, the teleport operator could program the device to remove a chuck of material. The piece removed could be exactly specified to allow a bug to be planted in that space. No drilling or cutting was necessary, and nothing had to be created to maintain an illusion that had to hide an opening in the wall, floor, ceiling, or in this case, the table. The bug could be teleported into the space precisely; no matter what happened, it would not give itself away.

Jake had only briefly considered putting a video bug into the room. He quickly dismissed the notion and chose an audio bug. The video bug would generate too much data to be easily disguised, whereas audio signals took up much less room. Jake also didn't think the video would be all that interesting, but what was said would be. He waited for Odin to report to him that the listening device was in place.

Once the work was done Jake let Odin know that he was ready to move on. A moment later he returned to the ship, and an instant later materialized in the executive lavatory. It was pretty much as he expected: well-lit, spacious, and full of expensive and gaudy fixtures. He aimed his perscomp at a spot on the ceiling part-way through the row of stalls. Less than a minute later he pocketed another bit of material; the second listening device was in place. Jake was back on his ship in time to catch the last three songs of Evvie's concert.

The first of three was a minor song of her latest release. The second was the number she usually closed with, and Jake thought that was the end. But shortly after the song was over and the applause had faded, Evvie said, "I want to do one last song. It's an oldie, and I hope you'll appreciate it." She nodded to her backup musicians. It took Jake precisely four seconds to recognize her closing song.

"Oh, my God. That's the *Marseilles*!"

"I believe you're correct, Jake," Odin observed.

"We're done for now! That stupid... Odin, take all standard security precautions, prepare for immediate teleport, and get the jump drive online."

"Absolutely. I am also initiating full monitoring of local security communications. I will alert you immediately."

"Stand by."

Jake watched the broadcast nervously. He wondered how long it would take for Maxis to catch on to what exactly Evvie was singing, and the underlying meaning of the anthem. She was able to get through the first verse of '*Marseilles*' without incident, but Jake was still on edge.

Evvie moved on to the next verse. As she sang and nothing happened, Jake relaxed just enough to break the tension with Odin. "Looks like she's doing a straight version of the song," he said.

"Yes, it would seem so."

"Funny that she hasn't brought in any of her usual pop stuff into it."

"True, but I would surmise that might be due to the song itself."

"What do you mean?"

"You are aware how sensitive the French-speaking peoples are with *Marseilles*. Or have you forgotten the scandal..."

"Oh, that's right."

Evvie completed the second verse without incident. When she came to the third, her backup singers and band members joined in, attempting to replicate the sound of a chorus. The effect was okay to Jake's mind, but simply couldn't compete with a trained classical chorus.

"Still," he said, "Evvie isn't a bad singer, really. I think if she challenged herself, and dropped some of the effects, she might be worth listening to."

Everyone more or less sailed through that verse and went right into the next. Jake started to wonder when the bottom was going to drop. Was Maxis letting them twist in the wind? Was it taking time to put his goons in place? Jake asked Odin about the situation. "Nothing unusual as yet," the computer reported.

Another verse came and went without trouble. On the following verse the chorus stopped, leaving just Evvie to sing. With the threat seeming to diminish, Jake was now getting anxious to have the thing over with.

"This song really goes on, doesn't it?"

"It is considered long for an anthem, Jake," Odin said. "Most people are only familiar with one verse of *Marseilles*. They see a drama where it is used, and assume that that one verse is the whole song. Interestingly, the same assumptions are made about the old American anthem *The Star-Spangled Banner*."

"Okay, fine. I was just making an observation. You don't have to go on at length to me, remember?"

"I am sorry."

"One might say you got carried away, there."

"You might. I would not."

Evvie completed her solo verse of '*Marseilles*,' then launched into another one. Despite his appreciation of higher culture, Jake found himself actually asking himself, "I don't know what's worse; waiting for this song to end, or waiting for Maxis to crack down on us." Evvie finished the verse without incident, said a few "thank you's," and jogged off the stage.

"That's it?"

"Apparently so," Odin replied. "I noticed that the audience

reaction was not quite as enthusiastic as usual."

"Maybe they got as antsy for the show to end as I was. Well, check with Evvie and see if she's ready to teleport. No sense taking any chances."

A minute later Odin reported on his communication with her. "It seems that Maxis wishes to speak to her personally. She doesn't want to disappoint him."

"She could be walking into danger."

"I am monitoring the situation, Jake. There doesn't appear to be any imminent threat. And might I point out that her not seeing him might alarm him in some way. This post-performance meeting was previously arranged, if you remember. Canceling it without an extremely convincing reason could create a new set of problems."

"Fine. Just keep monitoring."

Fifteen nervous minutes passed before Evvie contacted the ship and said she was ready to teleport up. Jake told Odin to operate the teleport while he dashed to the room. He arrived an instant after she materialized.

"Do you know the danger you put us into?" he demanded.

"What danger?"

"*Marseilles*, Evvie. If Maxis caught on to the meaning..."

"He didn't."

Jake was speechless for a moment. "What?"

Evvie shook her head. "He didn't get it. In fact, he told me he liked the song. He thought it sounded exotic. He said I should sing more songs like it."

"And he doesn't know the history of the *Marseilles*? He didn't give you any hints that he knows what the lyrics really mean?"

"Nope."

"And you didn't tell him, in some fit of grand stupidity?"

"Of course not."

Jake pondered the matter for several seconds. Finally, he shook his head and crossed his arms across his chest. "Well, then, I think we've just found someone more shallow and clueless than you," he said to Evvie. He turned and drifted away, still shaking his head.

***

Jake was still on edge the following morning. It wasn't so much out of fear than from annoyance. Evvie and Sid were still on board. He hadn't heard them get up, but by the time he entered the bridge after breakfast they were awake, cleaned up, filled up, and meeting behind the closed door of Evvie's room. He didn't know what they were talking about, but he was pretty sure when they told him he wouldn't like it.

Eventually Sid wandered onto the bridge. Evvie was not with him. "Jake, Evvie's taking some time to rest," Sid reported. "She's going to do some personal stuff today. I hope you don't mind."

"Just so long as she doesn't start talking to her friends about her new political sensibilities," Jake said.

"Oh, sure. She's just gonna rest her voice, take it easy, y'know."

"Fine."

"Say, Jake. I've been doing some thinking."

"Do tell." *I hope it didn't hurt.*

"This rebellion thing you're pulling, it's a great idea. But I was just wondering, do you think a little publicity's in order?"

"Uh, no. The whole point of the exercise is not to let Maxis know we're going to oust him from office."

"Oh, I get that. I mean, publicity to the wider galaxy."

Jake let out a long sigh. "Sid, if Maxis knows who Evvie is, don't you think he also pays attention to the news?"

"Well, I suppose. But still, Jake, everything could use some publicity. I mean, how do you know that this rebellion will go over well?"

"I don't care how it goes over, so long as it succeeds and I'm paid for my work. If you have to put any spin on it, save it until after it's over."

Sid smiled. It was a gesture that sent chills down Jake's spin. "But, Jakie, what if, in carrying out this rebellion thing, you do some things that don't go over well later on? See, that's what I was thinking about. I think you and those rebels might want to talk to a consultant."

"A consultant? There aren't any rebellion consultants."

"Uh-uh. You can find a consultant for just about any situation. See, I'll hire the guy, link him or her up to you, and you can let them give you tips on strategy, uniforms, all that stuff."

"No."

"But, Jake..."

"Listen." Jake raised his right hand and pointed his forefinger at the ceiling. "The computer that controls this ship is one of the few artificial intellingences in existence. Odin has access to every bit of information known to humanity. If we need any help on tactics or strategy, Odin will have no trouble finding an answer. He can sift through every military history, every biography or autobiography, every news account that currently exists.

"Now, as to uniforms... what uniforms? This revolution will not be televised. It will be quiet, held in secret, and will not make stars out of anyone until it is over and has ended well. What do you think is more important, looking good or getting the job done?

"No, don't answer that, you're not qualified.

"Now, I was the guy the Rosens hired. That means I am in charge of this little rebellion. You and Evvie can play ball my way, or you can leave the field. Am I clear?"

"I guess."

"Good. Now I think it's time my ship and yours got started for the next venue. Say good-bye to Evvie, Odin will beam you off, and we'll carry on like before. Okay?"

Sid nodded, but he obviously wasn't happy about having been shot down. He wandered off the bridge, leaving Jake to sit in silence for a few minutes. Odin finally broke the silence by reporting that Sid had been teleported to his ship. Jake ordered Odin to set a new course, and engage at his discretion.

"By the way, Jake," Odin said, "I appreciate your coming to my defense."

"Well, it was either that or deal with Sid's consultants. You may be a little frustrating at times, but you aren't an idiot. I'd rather be frustrated by brains than by stupidity."

***

Jake no longer bothered to count how many times he had sat on the bridge while Evvie was interviewed. With the tour now in its final lap, this was just minor annoyance to be endured. Once or twice more, he told himself, and he would be on the path to real wealth.

But this interview was slightly different. After the usual banal greeting Evvie said, "I want to let everyone know that the last three shows of my tour are dedicated to the ideal of liberty."

"Really?" the interviewer asked.

Jake coughed in surprise.

"That's right. Lots of us take it for granted. But I don't. I'm glad I'm free to sing what I want to. I'm glad that my fans are free to hear my songs. I'd like all of us throughout known space to have this freedom."

"That's a very admirable sentiment, Evvie. What brought it on?"

"Well, getting out, traveling to all sorts of worlds. We sometimes don't think about other people, what with our busy lives and all. I've had my eyes opened about what's going on. I want to do my part, and I want my fans to help do theirs, too."

Jake gritted his teeth as the interview wound through its final moments. When it was over and the screen darkened he leapt from his seat. "Are you a complete idiot?" he snapped. "No, don't bother answering. I know what you'll say."

"What are you so bugged about, Jake?"

"You really don't have to dedicate your last couple shows to liberty. It would be better if you didn't."

"But you kept making fun of me for not saying anything important."

He sighed. "But you don't have to say what you said."

"But my fans need to hear that."

"Including that one really big fan on Antioch Two? You remember? The one we're supposed to oust from power?"

"Yeah. So?"

"So, if he hears you, and puts two and two together,..." Jake waited for her to catch on. She didn't. "He might take action that could endanger our chances of success, Evvie. Lock people up. Tighten security. Make our job harder."

"Oh."

"Yeah, oh. Do me a favor. Look up the word 'subtle.' Try to understand that word before your next interview. Employ the concept when you're tempted to talk about liberty."

Evvie glared at him for a second, then turned and left the bridge. Jake took a few breaths to calm himself, walked back up to the stairs, and went back to watching the latest remake of a **A Tale of Two Cities**.

Seven
Villainous Inefficiency

As he sat down in the chair in the upper section of the bridge, Jake let out a long sigh of relief. "Okay, Odin. We're going to have a little bit of peace, so let's get put it to good use."

"Evvie and Sid?"

"Saying their oh-so-sincere goodbyes to the rest of the hired help. Followed by a meeting with each parent separately, then a few interviews. She won't be back on board until tomorrow."

"How do you plan to celebrate?"

"Loudly. Tonight. For now I want to know what's the latest you've found out about Antioch Two. Then I'd like us to put all the pieces together before we get bombarded with silly questions. Besides, I'm going to need the information to figure out how exactly we're going to help the Rosens and boot this Maxis character out."

"Very well. Any preference as to where I begin?"

"Start with that main dome."

"Certainly. My analysis is not yet complete, but only one or two items remain to be verified."

A two-dimensional image of the main dome of Antioch Two appeared on the largest screen on the console in front of Jake. There were six levels to the dome, as both already knew. As he described each room on each level, Odin posted a written label onto each relevant part of the image.

"I have confirmed much of what the Rosens told us. The top level is, as we've long suspected, where the control over the planet and its resources is wielded. There is one main control room, a medium-sized robot repair shop, and the executive meeting room. In addition, there is also a separate reception area, and the living quarters for Maxis and his senior staff."

Odin devoted a second screen to two-dimensional images of the actual rooms assembled from security camera shots. Jake took some time to switch his gaze from one screen to the other. He immediately noticed that the rooms were as bland as the planet they were located on. The walls of work rooms were painted in good old battleship gray, the others a tan shade of off-white. The floors of the work rooms were covered by white tile, the others by yellowish-white carpet. The ceilings of all the rooms were out-and-out white. Only the executive meeting room seemed spacious; Jake thought the living quarters weren't too many square meters bigger than his room on the ship.

The accessories in the rooms were just as boring as the decor. Consoles and equipment in the work spaces were gray, tan, metallic silver, metallic black, or beige. The furniture appeared to be wood-shaded plastic, except for the table in the executive meeting room which appeared to be real wood. There was a bit more coloring in the personal living quarters, but the choices and styles seemed unimaginative to Jake.

All that's missing, he thought, *are old-fashioned particleboard cubicles.*

"Did you find out where the staff works?" he asked.

"Yes, in that control room, apparently on some sort of rotational schedule. The staff seems to divide their work time between there and the various external operations."

"Doesn't sound like a good use of their time."

"It isn't."

An idea popped into Jake's head. "You think Maxis might be doing that intentionally? Keeping some there and some out to prevent them from spending too much time together?"

"For what purpose?"

"You know, to keep them from making plans behind his back."

"Oh, I see. I hadn't considered that possibility."

"It makes sense, in a dictatorial kind of way."

"Yes, it does. I see that the Rosens were again correct in hiring us."

"Me. You don't use credits, remember?"

"Shall I continue? Thank you. The second level is indeed devoted to living quarters for the forepersons, the cafeteria, child care and education, and a sickbay. Levels three through five are for workers' living quarters."

Odin again provided security-cam images of the rooms and corridors in question. The larger rooms all had the same corporate decor that the official rooms on the first level had, except that there was no wood and more plastic. The sample living space shown was about a third smaller than the spaces given to the executives. Only

73

the child care center and the school rooms had any signs of real life and color, and that came more from manufactured images than from children's drawings. Even the corridors in the dome seemed cramped and dull.

"Which brings us to level six and the mystery rooms the Rosens mentioned."

"Correct. The smaller room next to the vehicle boarding area is a reserve control room with elevator access to all levels. The only times it appears to be manned is during boarding, and when repairs have to be conducted on equipment in main control.

"The larger room next to boarding, and adjacent to reserve control, is a large robot repair shop. This shop has very sophisticated machinery for diagnostics and repair, all automated. Records indicate that if a guardbot requires major repairs, only Thorne and one senior staff person will supervise the work in this shop. Records also indicate that only Maxis and Thorne have the appropriate clearance to enter this room."

"Interesting." Jake rubbed his chin. "Any way you can thwart that?"

"Not without their cooperation. The security program uses a combination of retina, thumbprint, DNA, and full-body scans to make identification. Furthermore, the program cannot accept modifications in its code without making an actual scan of the coder, which of course is either Maxis or Thorne."

"You can't even spoof it?"

"No. Which actually is quite interesting, since most of the other systems, including those which control the refinery and the gold and silver storage units, do not have security blocks so severe as in this repair shop. Maxis must believe that guardbot control is his one weak spot."

"That, or he doesn't care who swipes the gold so long as he stays in charge. Anything else on level six, Odin?"

"Yes. On the opposite side of the boarding area is the food and water processing plant. It appears to be fully automated. There are some systems in this area that I have yet to identify completely. I wish to confirm the information before making any statements."

"Okay." *Odd*, Jake thought. *Odin wouldn't hedge like that.* "So that's the main dome. Were you able to confirm the existence of the other domes?"

"I was. Allow me to show you."

Odin changed the screen from the dome display to a surface map. The dome was placed in the center of the map and colored green. Surrounding it at a distance and mainly to its north and east were yellow blobs. Over each blob was a red dot. Three blue dots appeared close to the dome, while a purple one appeared well beyond the dome.

"The yellow areas are the veins presently being exploited. The red dots indicated the mine entrances. The blue dot one kilometer west of the dome is the reclamation plant. The blue dot two kilometers south is the supply dome and transfer pad. The last blue dot, two kilometers northeast, is the mineral processing plant."

"And that purple one?"

"A small security dome, not staffed. The computer and transmitter that relay orders to the guardbots is located here."

Odin followed the map with images taken from the ship while in orbit. Oddly enough, or perhaps not, these places looked much more interesting than the rooms in the main dome. The plants were steel boxes and cylinders of various sizes that shared walls or were connected by dark blue tubing. The transit pad was concrete white with black scorch marks and signs of chipping. The supply dome was actually a massive light blue and gray warehouse with white doors. The vehicles trudging around the facilities were all bright yellow, and everything was linked to each other and the main dome by ribbons of black.

After looking at the images and the map for a few minutes Jake noticed how far the tiny security dome was from everything else. "That dome seems awfully far away to keep control," he said.

"In point of fact, contact between it, main control, and reserve control is maintained through wireless communications. Distance does not matter."

"Hm. Could we blast it from space, or bomb it, to take the actual facility out of action?"

"Such attacks would not be effective. I was able to uncover the security protocols for these systems. If contact is lost between the dome and the guardbots, either through interference or because the facility is damaged or destroyed, the guardbots will immediately alert main control. At that point one of two actions will occur. Either a software backup system will take control, or the guardbots will be operated with some manual control."

"I assume that also at that point there would be some sort of a lockdown of everyone in the dome."

"I was unable to find any such plans, but your assumption is reasonable."

"So how are we supposed to knock out those bots? Blast them one by one? That could get messy, especially if they're equipped with self-defense programming."

"I agree. Perhaps this is not the time to attempt to solve such a problem."

"Yeah, I guess so." Jake let out a breath. "Well, at least this won't be a complete walk in the park. We'll have to do some real work. And speaking of work, Odin, what does Maxis do while everyone else is slaving away to make him rich?"

"Not much, it seems. I didn't dig deep into his schedule, but from what I did gather he workload is extremely light. There are daily meetings with his staff, the occasional visit to workers, calls to various persons off-world, and very little else."

"I see. You are saving all the data you collect, true?"

"Of course."

"Good. We may need to use these tidbits to get public support for this revolt."

"In that case, Jake, I have another such 'tidbit' for you. I uncovered the reason why Antioch Two is the personal property of Sordius Maxis."

Jake leaned back in his seat. "Is this a good story?"

"I believe it will appeal to all your baser emotions."

"Tell me the whole sordid story."

"First, you must understand that I've compiled this chain of events from several sources, not simply from the planetary archives. You might say that I have assembled pieces of a puzzle. Although not all the pieces are present, there were more than enough to make a coherent picture."

As he narrated the tale, Odin displayed a series of images on the screen as he spoke. First were photos of the man Jake saw in one of the paintings in the executive meeting room. After that was an employment record, several news-net stories, and a corporate planetary report on the mineral wealth of Antioch Two.

The painting in the executive room portrayed an imperious and imposing older man. Flecks of gray shaded his dark hair, and grim intelligence radiated from his dark blue eyes. The news images showed a slightly younger and much less imposing person. His clothes seemed to hang off him just a bit. His face was mild, his body average, and his style spoke of a man scraping by. Jake had no trouble guessing that this was the founder of the current Maxis family of scoundrels.

"This chain of events goes back to Maxis' grandfather His name was Morgan Maxi," Odin said, pronouncing the name as 'max-eye.' "Maxi was a senior mineral geologist with Interstellar Resources Management. At the time he arrived on Antioch Two, he was under investigation by four planetary governments for taking bribes in exchange for altering reports. Some alterations were in favor of his employer, while others would have been in the favor of property owners. Aside from an increasing scale of bribes, there was no other pattern to the alterations."

"So bribery is an inheritance of the family?" Jake asked. "Interesting. Continue."

"I was able to locate Maxi's report to IRM on the mineral wealth of Antioch Two. It does not in any way conform to the facts as we know them. Maxi grossly underestimated the exploitation potential of the planet, and in turn overestimated the planetary trends towards biological evolution. Maxi had all the proper equipment when making his survey, and records indicate that it was working normally."

"So any oversight on his part was clearly intentional?"

"The evidence suggests precisely that."

"Maxi was being investigated. I take it he avoided being indicted or convicted?"

"He did. IRM arranged for his early retirement in exchange for his testimony against the accused local officials. He was not the main target of the probe, but a target of opportunity. The various planetary prosecutors at the time all believed that with Maxi retired, he was unlikely to further violate the law."

Jake smiled. "Let me guess. They were so off they were in orbit."

"They were proved wrong, yes. Shortly after Maxi testified, IRM decided not to exercise its option to colonize Antioch Two. Ownership was therefore placed on the open market. The highest bid, and indeed the only bid, came from a private firm, Maxwell and Morgan. This firm consisted of Maxi and his twenty-three-year-old son."

"Surprise, surprise."

"For the next five years they recruited workers. These workers were presented with a complicated employee contract with two extremely unpleasant stipulations. First, any costs of child care and youth education are deducted from parents' pay. This has had the effect of severely limited family size to two children, with fore-persons able to afford three. Second, there is a nondisclosure clause written so broadly that resigning from employment is considered a contract violation."

"And I'll bet children are held to that clause once they're old enough."

"With the consequences to themselves and their parents fully explained."

"Well, that explains alot. So how did 'Maxi' become 'Maxis?'"

"With Morgan's son. He was given the first name 'Darius.'"

"So who was Maxwell?"

"'Maxwell' was his middle name."

"And no doubt used to cover up the funny business."

"Probably true. At any rate, I found records on Antioch Two of punishments being doled out for mispronouncing both Darius' first and last name. Obviously this was a sensitive matter to him. After his father died he had the 's' added, perhaps because of this."

Odin showed images of Darius that were probably buried in the planetary archive. Whereas the painting in the meeting room showed a middle-aged man with dark brown hair and a confident demeanor, the images spoke of a nervous fellow desperate for respect. Most of the images were of Darius yelling, waiting, or standing uncomfortably at some event.

It had been several decades since Antioch Two had been bought, Jake noticed. Morgan was unlikely to be still alive, and since Sordius was clearly in control, Darius had to be in retirement. Jake idly wondered if Sordius was ripping off his father.

He shook his head. *No, his dad's probably living his own good life off his own ill-gotten gains.*

Which leads to an obvious question. "Where the Hell did Darius come up with the name 'Sordius' for his son?"

"Originally Sordius' first name was 'Tiberius.' It was changed when he turned seventeen. There are traces of a search of the names and biographies of old Roman emperors made just before that point."

"Venture any conclusions, Odin?"

"Absolutely not. You may speculate if you like."

"Okay." Jake took several seconds to think. "I suppose he didn't find any names right. If he took a good emperor he'd be compared to him. A name of a bad one would remind everyone of their situation. I guess he tried coming up with his own Roman-sounding name, and 'Sordius' sounded good."

"Your reasoning seems logical."

"Is that all the dirt? Or does Sordius have any other skeletons in his closet?"

"I have no more *gossip* for you, Jake. But I do have additional facts. Facts that should further encourage the Rosens. The, shall we say, management of the planet's mines is not producing peak output. According to my estimates, production has not been at peak efficiency for at least four decades."

"Maxis' iron rule isn't producing results? Odin, I'm shocked."

"Your sarcasm is most appropriate. I take it you've been reading again."

Jake smiled blandly. "Long before we met, I knew enough history to know that dictatorships are rarely efficient. Aside from their other faults, of course."

"Then you will also not be surprised to learn that the amount of minerals removed from the planet does not correlate to the amount sold."

"What? Maxis is hoarding gold and silver?"

"There may be some of that. I cannot say for certain, since there does not appear to be any place on the planet to store minerals, much less to form them into blocks, bricks, bars, or the like. I think is it much more reasonable to conclude that this error is due to outdated refining equipment. Indeed, much of the machinery is at least two decades old. Any modernization carried out has been to the mining machinery and the guardbots."

"Let me guess; everything else is secondhand, bought cheap on the resale market, or held together with the proverbial duct tape and chewing gum?"

"Correct."

"Doesn't Maxis understand any of this?"

"I cannot answer that question, Jake."

"No, I was wondering if his staff have bothered to point out any of this."

"Again, I cannot say. I could attempt to access the minutes of the executive meetings. Perhaps someone has brought up these shortcomings."

"Perhaps someone has, and he isn't happy about not being listened to."

"And possibly turned against Maxis," Odin added. "Clever thinking."

"Thank you. It seems we've got some motivation beyond greed and sympathy. The Rosens and their people need our help to maximize output. Accountant logic in service of a rebellion." Jake shook his head. "What is the universe coming to?"

"I would not even hazard a reply, Jake."

"You're too stuck up, Odin. You need to occasionally get down in the dirt with the rest of us."

"I think not. I have been analyzing the transmissions from the device we planted in the executive lavatory. The 'dirt,' as you put it, is not place for any sentient being, organic or artificial."

"What, those bugs are paying off? Show me."

"If I must."

Odin put on the screen in front of Jake a log of entrances and exits of the senior staff to the bathroom, and the conversations that were recorded. The most interesting thing Jake found was that conversations were actually few and far between. It might have simply been an anomaly for the period, but it appeared that few of Maxis' lackeys went to the john in pairs or groups.

Unfortunately, those that did had very little interesting to say to each other. The log entries has such scintillating titles as "Evvie's Concert," "Family Boasts," "Personal Investment Advice," and the always-political "Interpersonal Sexual Relations." Essentially, Maxis and his cronies were just as shallow and gossip-obsessed as any other group of corporate hacks. If there was any behind-the-scenes talk of a more incendiary nature, it was going on elsewhere, Jake concluded.

"Or it could be that Maxis' senior staff fear being overheard there," Odin suggested. "That is a typical human response to absolute authority."

"Your scans didn't locate any bugs before I teleported down."

"True."

"Have you found purchase orders for concealed recording devices?"

"No."

"So, while his staff might be fearful, it could just as well be true that they're just as shallow as the next business suit."

"In that case, Jake, I must ask, is this a revolution or a management change?"

Jake smiled. "Every revolution is a change of management, when you get right down to it."

"That is quite a cynical statement."

"Cynical, yes. But I don't hear you disputing it accuracy."

The room was silent for a moment. "Why, Odin, it seems that prolonged exposure to me is rubbing off on you. Maybe I'm not the only one benefitting from our little partnership after all."

***

The next day Evvie returned to the ship to start her new career as a revolutionary. Before taking them to Antioch Two, Jake had her sit down next to him on the couch. "I think you need to know why this revolution is important to those people," he told her.

"Well, isn't that obvious? They need to be free?"

"Yes, well, that's true. But there are more solid reasons for doing this. The situation is a little more complicated that just an evil ruler oppressing his people."

"Complicated?"

Jake raised a hand. "I'll explain it to you in terms you can understand, okay?"

"Okay."

"Great. Now, first of all, the planet is Maxis' personal property."

"Is that legal? I thought you couldn't buy planets. I mean, I tried, once, but..."

Jake cleared his throat. "May I continue?"

"Oh, sorry."

"Thank you. In point of fact, no, you can't buy planets. At least not planets that have potential, like Antioch Two and its mineral wealth. You see, Evvie, Maxis' grandfather lied to his employers about the value of the planet's potential, and he proceeded to buy it at auction. Instead of owning some worthless rock, he bought one of the richest worlds in human space for almost nothing."

"Sounds bad."

"It was beyond bad. It was illegal. Now the world and its wealth belongs to one person, Sordius Maxis. What's more, Maxis is paying bribes all over the galaxy to hide this fact, to hide how badly he treats the people working for him, and to hide some of his other schemes to fatten his bank accounts. And on top of all that, the way he operates his planet isn't as good as it should be."

"Isn't that obvious? He's a dictator."

"No, not in the way you're thinking. His equipment is old, his refinery isn't turning out as much as it should or could, and the way he keeps everyone in line is limiting how much everyone could be making from such a mineral-rich planet."

"Oh. Still sounds like a bad man to me."

"He is, Evvie. The point is he's bad in more than just the usual ways."

"Okay, well, that's fine. What are we going to do about it?"

"We're going to oust him from power."

"How? I mean, are we gonna just blast him from space?"

"No. We can't shoot him from space."

"Why not? I mean, if he's the problem..."

"For one thing, we couldn't pick him off like that. Not while he's in the dome. Either we'd hurt people we don't want to, or we'd miss and alert him that we were there. Besides, this isn't about getting one man. There's a system that we have to get rid of. That's why this is a 'revolution' and not a 'coup.'"

"So what do we do?"

"Well, we get the people to want Maxis out. We undermine his leadership, and tell the people under him what's really going on."

"That doesn't sound very exciting, Jake."

"Don't worry. It will get exciting as time goes on. I know patience isn't one of your virtues, Evvie, but you will have to be patient. And you will have a role to play, I assure you."

"Great. Just so long as it doesn't involve boring stuff."

Jake sighed. *What have I gotten myself into?*

Eight
Revolutions For Dummies

"Are you certain she's busy?" Jake asked Odin.

"I am assisting her, Jake. Contact the Rosens."

"Right."

Jake didn't usually open connections on his own; he let Odin take care of that. But this time the computer was busy helping Evvie learn a fact or two about waging revolutions. Fortunately Jake wasn't a complete novice, and Odin had left a clear path to follow. In moments the Rosens appeared on the small screen in front of him.

"I've got some good news, and some not so good news," he began. "The good news is my other job is done. At this moment my ship is in orbit over Antioch Two. It's now time to get the ball rolling."

"Thank goodness," Clarissa said with obvious relief.

"The not so good news is I have a partner. Evvie Martini, to be precise."

"Evvie's going to help us?"

"In a limited capacity. I had to agree to let her help to keep her people from talking about this."

"Oh, well, that's fine. I think we'd be excited to have a big star like hers on our side."

"If you say so. Oh, I had to let her take the media rights to the story."

"What story?"

"This story. The story of the revolution."

"Oh. Well, I don't think that will be a problem."

"So long as we're free," Daniel added.

"If you say so," Jake said. "Okay, the reason for this call is simple. We need to figure out how we're going to carry out this revolution."

"What's to figure out?" Clarissa asked. "We fight Maxis until we win."

"How do we fight him?"

"What about weapons?" Daniel asked.

"What about them?" Jake responded.

"Well, aren't you going to get us any? Do we have to buy them?"

Jake's first thought was to tell Daniel that he didn't trust the younger man with anything more lethal than paper. But that would be far too rude. Tempting as it was to verbally smack the couple around, Jake didn't want to hurt his big chance at permanent semiretirement.

"You said to fight," he said to the couple. "Fight who, specifically?"

"Well, Maxis and cronies."

"The guardbots," Clarissa added.

"Okay. Now, you can't shoot at a guardbot from the front. It will see you carrying and fire first. Right?"

"Oh, right." Daniel's face lit up. "We shoot them from behind!"

"Okay, so you shoot one from behind and take it out. Don't you think Maxis and his pals are going to notice that someone's blasted one of his guardbots? Don't you think that's going to make him a wee bit suspicious?"

"Oh, yeah, I guess so."

"Now, suppose you decide you're going to go after all the guardbots at once. When are you going to do that? Are you going to have a few dozen people not show up at their jobs one day? Wouldn't that be suspicious?"

"Well, what about at night?" Clarissa asked.

"The guardbots don't sleep," Jake replied. "The first one shot will set off alarms. Or do you plan to sneak all these people into position, at night, to take out every bot? How exactly are you going to accomplish this without anyone in main control noticing all this movement?"

"We could rise up at lunch, or..." Daniel's face fell. "Oh. We'd only be on one level."

Jake smiled. "There you go. Maxis could just call up guardbots from the other levels to fight it out with you. Now do you start to see the problem?"

"So how are we going to fight?"

"There won't be any fighting. It's too risky. Think about this: some people might not side with you if you start shooting bots, let alone shooting real human beings. They might even decide to fight against you. And don't forget, shooting and missing can create damage. You don't want to start your new regime by sinking what few credits you have into repair and replacement costs, do you?

"No, there are just too many risks with staging a violent revolt. If we're to install a nicer leadership we'll have to do it with peaceful, nonviolent methods of revolution."

"Okay," Daniel said, "so what would those methods be?"

"Well, first of all we've got to get the people riled up. We've got some final scans to do up here; maybe they'll give us a tactic to employ. The next thing we'll do try to undermine Maxis' control."

"Labor actions?"

"No. I think a little propaganda might be in order. Let me tell you two something. Maxis isn't just a repressive ruler. He's also a corrupt con artist who's tossing bribes right and left. You remember I asked you about what happens to retirees? Well, Maxis and the retirement center your seniors move to are ripping off you and the authorities, and making a fat file of credits in the bargain. Odin and I have uncovered several other schemes like that one."

"So how does that help us?"

"Maxis is getting rich at your expense. Doesn't that make you mad?"

"You're right, it does."

"Here's something else to make you mad. Your mining and refining operations are using old equipment. If Maxis spent a little more on that, instead of lining his pockets, you'd have a more productive operation."

"And if he wasn't treating us like rocks," Clarissa said, "we'd be making more and living better lives."

"Precisely. We'll not only get that message out, but we'll repeat it over and over until the people are so pissed off that rallying them won't be a problem. And we'll use that message to get someone in Maxis' inner circle on our side. Once everything's nice and unstable, we'll give a small push, and that'll be that."

"Great. So what do we do?"

"Be patient for a little longer. Give me a few days to put a few things in order, and start undermining Maxis from our end. Don't do anything until I tell you to."

"It is our revolution."

"Yes, *ours*, Clarissa. Mine as well as yours. Follow my lead, and I promise this will end up the way you want it to. Okay?"

"Okay, Jake."

"Good. Hang on, and I'll be in touch. Bye."

As the image of the Rosens faded, Jake thought, *Now to figure out how to get this particular ball rolling.*

***

The next morning Jake was in the lower part of the bridge, angrily tapping his foot. Behind him on the large bridge screen was a three-dimensional view of the main dome on Antioch Two. It had been five minutes since he's asked his partner to join him, and Evvie still hadn't appeared. "Call her again," he asked Odin.

"I'm here," she said as she walked up. "I had to get ready. Jeez, Jake, don't you know it takes women time to get themselves ready to face the day?"

Jake sighed. "Just sit down, and pay attention to the screen."

"What is that?"

"The layout of the main dome."

"Nice. The colors are a bit bland. And I have seen those projections before."

"Evvie, sit down."

"Why?"

"It's part of waging a revolution, Evvie. It's called 'mission planning.' We sit, we look at this, and we try to figure out what to do first."

"Why do I have to be here?"

"You want the publicity, you have to participate."

Evvie heaved a sigh then sat down. She glanced at the image for exactly one second. "Where's the armory?"

"They don't have one," Jake said.

"Why not?"

"The guardbots."

"Oh. So there aren't any guards we can bribe? No weapons we can take?"

"No."

"Maxis does have a personal guard," Odin added, "but it only consists of twelve persons, and only four are on duty per shift. These persons appear to be armed with sidearms. I found no traces of heavy weaponry."

"As could be expected," Jake said.

"What about the drug plant?" Evvie asked. "Y'know, where they make the drugs to suppress the rebelling urges in the people?"

86

Jake rolled his eyes. *Well, at least she's managed to do some research about revolutions after agreeing to help. Too bad for her "research" is watching hokey old videos and not reading actual history.*

"Evvie, something like that only occurs in fiction. Reality is not like that."

"Actually, Jake, you are incorrect," Odin interrupted. "I call your attention to that large room on level six."

"That's food processing."

"Yes. I previously discovered hardware and software tied into the main food processing systems. I investigated these thoroughly. They are used for the specific purpose of injecting chemicals into a food supply system."

That explains why Odin hedged a couple days ago, Jake mused.

"Such systems are typical of mental institutions housing dangerous individuals," Odin continued. "They prevent ordinary nurses, visitors, and other unqualified personnel from being placed in threatening situations. They are admirable safety measures, accepted by every civilized government."

"Okay. What are they doing here?"

"Since there are no facilities for housing the mentally ill, the only logical conclusion is that these systems are used to inject chemicals into the workers' food and drink."

"Y'see?" Evvie said.

Jake ignored her. "So what chemical or chemicals are being injected, Odin?"

"I was able to uncover shipping records for only one chemical. The medical name for the substance is Lypinisan Oh-Five. The more common name is 'Relaxafin.'"

"Oh, my God."

"What?" Evvie asked.

"Relaxafin. Those commercials? Y'know, the hokey ones with those formerly hyperactive kids being all nice and quiet?" He impersonated the actress who played the grateful mother in the spots. "'It's given my child his peace back.'" He then did eerily passive kid. "'I can work with others now.'" He shook his head. "Those commercials have consistently been criticized by almost everyone as the worst broadcast spots for four years running."

"By who? I mean, they work, don't they?"

"Only in the cheesiest, stupidest way possible. The only campaign that anywhere close to being that annoying is the one for that colonial building chain that uses that beaver."

Evvie shuddered visibly. "Don't mention that, please. That beaver creeps me out. I once had this dream..."

"Please. No."

"But..."

"No. Odin, is Maxis using that operation for what I think he's using it for?"

"It appears that it's being used to repress anger, and therefore to repress any unrest or dissension."

"Is this drug being injected in dangerous amounts?"

"Actually, it's being used in dosages well below average, and only in the adult population. That suggests the drug is being used as a minor control on the population's mental state. I should add that Relaxafin is comparatively expensive. That might also be a factor in the small dosages used."

"Geez. He can't be a little more imaginative?"

"What do you mean?"

"Never mind. Odin, what might happen if the people stop taking their current doses of Relaxafin?"

"Nothing for roughly three to four weeks. Studies show it takes about that long for the human body to circulate out prolonged exposure to the drug. Then from four to six weeks after ingestion has stopped, the body's adrenaline flow increases to higher than normal levels. In human beings this increase lasts from three to five days. At that point the mental state returns to a more normal pattern."

Jake shook his head and pondered the situation. *What happens when life begins to imitate art? When the bad guys don't come up with original ways to hurt people, but instead rely on ancient videos and stereotypes for their strategies? When everyone's acting, even when they're living real life?*

Do I really want an answer to those questions? No. They're giving me a headache and a profound sense of despair.

And anyway, if Maxis isn't smart enough to figure out what a stereotype he is, he won't see the end coming. That means beating an idiot.

Maybe this state of affairs isn't as bad as it seems.

Evvie finally broke his train of thought by saying, "Okay, so we hit that plant. It's gonna take awhile for people to get angry. What do we do until then?"

When in Rome, Jake thought, *speak with a English accent.* "We rally the populace to our side. But first things first. You said you wanted to take part in this revolution. Well, I can't take out that plant on my own."

"I don't know. I mean, I'm not supposed to get myself into any danger."

"Okay. I'm sure one of the Rosens could help. Of course, the video will have to accurately reflect their help in this attack and not yours. But I'm sure..."

"Hold it. You mean if I stay out you'll insist that I be kept out when the video gets shot?"

Jake smiled. "Lack of accuracy in drama is not tolerated, Evvie. Unless you don't mind getting bad reviews for fudging the facts."

Evvie nodded firmly. "As long as I'm not in any serious danger, I think I should go and help you out. Y'know, do my part. I mean, I did sign on. Gotta take some risks for freedom and all that, right?"

***

Jake once heard someone in some forum say without fear of contradiction, "Technology creates more problems than it solves." But in his experience the reverse was just as true: tech solved as many problems as it created. That was certainly the case when he and Evvie took out the drug injection system.

The first problem was that of the lone guard in main control. The guard had in front of him a variety of displays and screens to observe what went on throughout the domes of the planet. Among those screens was one connected to the cameras trained on the food processing plant, where the injection system was located.

Actually, this part presented two problems. The first was the guard himself, and the second the data stream from the cameras. The second was the easiest to deal with. Odin could access the control system, intercept the data stream, and send a new stream down the pipe that showed nothing going on. That way no one reviewing the data later would see the attack on the equipment. But there would be a pause of a second or two as Odin cut into the stream, and the guard could spot such a pause and get suspicious.

Luckily it was the just the one man to deal with, and the ship was equipped to handle such situations. In the inventory was a mechabug, an artificial insect designed and built for stealthy operations. Among the mechabug's uses was spraying things into the air. Jake had sleeping gas put into its tiny container, and programmed it to spread the gas once it materialized.

"Do they have bugs down there?" Evvie asked as Jake placed the device on the teleport platform.

"Doesn't matter. It will appear under the guard's chair. It flies without making noise, and it's smart enough not to let it be seen. The guy won't know it's there."

Jake teleported the tiny machine down to the control room. He tapped into a motion sensor on the mechabug and waited. About five minutes later the sensor indicated that the guard's head had moved downward towards the console in front of him. Jake turned on an audio sensor; the sound of nasal snoring blared over the sound system.

"Phase one complete," he said. "Time for phase two."

He brought the mechabug back to the ship and teleported it to its place in the armory. He handed Evvie his perscomp, and together they stepped onto the platform.

"New data stream being transmitted," Odin reported.

"Very well. Send us down."

Jake and Evvie materialized in the food processing center. Jake glanced around, looking for the guardbot. When he found it he motioned to Evvie. The two of them quietly approached the robot as it carried out its night patrol.

The guardbot would not have scared anyone had they walked up on it from behind, as Jake and Evvie did. It was a meter-tall gray cylinder with four small wheels surrounding a single tread. Looking at it from that direction, a person might have assumed it was a prop robot from an ancient movie, replete with remote controls and a sound generator.

Only when it turned around did it look more serious. Two centimeters from the cylinder top was a red light. It was the housing for the bot's sensor array. The light wasn't essential, but generations of studies had proved that a robot with a red light near the top was more threatening than one with no light, or with a different color of light. Ten centimeters below the light was a stubby black finger signifying the bot's stun blaster. The edge of the finger started to turn blue when it turned to face Jake and Evvie.

Jake nodded at Evvie and towards the bot. Evvie nodded back, and tapped the screen of Jake's perscomp.

The bot's program immediately noticed the two intruders and was about to order the blaster to fire. But the bot received its orders over the air, and another part of its programming told it to inquire first before shooting, in case this was a surprise inspection. Jake had set up his perscomp to transmit instructions to the bot over the frequency it was expecting its new orders. The instructions were simple: Jake and Evvie were indeed carrying out an inspection, and the bot should not interfere with them. Unaware it was being lied to, the guardbot turned away from the two and went back to its patrol routine.

Jake nodded in satisfaction to Evvie. She handed the perscomp to him. He gave her a small device that looked like a pistol. He pointed to a corner of the large room. Evvie headed in that direction, while he walked to the injection equipment.

Jake suspected that a weapons discharge might set off an alarm, so vaporizing the drug supply was out of the question. His next thought was to let Evvie coat a corrosive agent onto the supply. He thought better of it when he realized that she do more damage with something like that. His final choice was to give her a sonic injector loaded with an agent that would render the lypinisan-05 ineffective.

He had a similar conundrum when trying to figure out how to disable the drug injection system. The solution was so obvious that he was slightly ashamed that it hadn't occurred to him immediately. He shut the system down, took a fine-point laser-drill from his belt, and used it to fry several tiny but extremely crucial, and expensive to replace, parts.

Within ten minutes Jake and Evvie had completed their tasks. They teleported back to the ship. Evvie went immediately to bed, while Jake put away the tools. When he was done he told Odin to monitor the listening device in the executive meeting room, and he went to sleep.

The next day Odin reported that the subject of the injection system was the sole topic of an executive meeting set for two hours before dinner. Jake took a seat at his chair on the upper deck of the bridge. Evvie sat down next to him, and on cue the device began broadcasting the meeting to them.

"We have a serious problem," one of the executives, a man

named Thorne, told the others. "It seems that last night our drug injection equipment was damaged."

"Sabotaged?" one the executives asked.

"I'm not sure. Some pretty vital parts were burned, maybe by a laser. The guardbot's log shows that two people were in the room during the night. But the video doesn't show anything out of the ordinary."

"Was the video tampered with?" Maxis asked.

"I don't think so. I couldn't see any traces of tampering, and the feed seems okay. But I have to believe that something did happen."

"Can we replace the damaged parts?"

"We can, sir, but it'll take a standard month to get them ordered and shipped out here."

"So do it."

"Sir, these parts are pretty expensive. Look at these numbers I printed out." There was the sound of Thorne handing Maxis sheets of paper.

"Ah."

"Yes, sir. The cost eats up most of this quarter's repair budget."

"We've already budgeted that to upgrade the silver extraction equipment," another executive said.

"I know," Maxis snapped. "We can't take care of this, and do that upgrade."

"I don't think we should postpone that upgrade, sir," Thorne said. "Silver is definitely trending up now. We'll need that upgrade to maximize revenue."

"Stef, what's the impact of the system going down?"

"Nothing for about a month," answered a woman who sounded a bit too young to be an executive, "then adrenaline rises for about a week."

"Would increased work prevent any problems?"

"I think so."

"Then it seems we have a solution," Maxis told the others. "We'll cut fifteen minutes to the work schedule, starting next week, then add fifteen more starting three weeks later. We'll explain it by saying we'll use the increased revenue to do that upgrade. Thorne, draft a memo to that effect. Tina, get the order for those parts sent in tomorrow."

"Sir, we may also have to order more lypinisan-05. The supply seems tampered with. I'll have to run some tests to make sure."

"Damn. Okay, Ross, test the supply. Find out how much we'll need, and how much a new supply will cost us. Check the generic suppliers. Maybe if we can find a cheaper source, we can persuade OmniPharmaCo to lower their price to us. The rest of you, look for places to temporarily cut costs. Our positions are on the line here, along with our income. Since the day's almost over, and not everything can be done at night, we'll hold this matter over until the day after tomorrow, morning meeting. We are adjourned." Everyone rose from their seats without talking and quickly left the room.

"Okay, Odin, that's enough." Jake turned to Evvie. "Well,..." Her eyes were shut. "Wake up!"

"I'm not sleeping."

"Then what were you doing?"

"Resting. That was boring, Jake. Bor-ring!"

"Oh, really? Odin, tell Evvie what she missed."

"Maxis' reaction to this situation was both predictable and inefficient. Rather than absorb a loss of profits to resolve the problem, he chose to employ accounting tricks, and to shift the burden onto the workers."

"So?" Evvie asked.

"So," Jake said, "Maxis is behaving like a typical bad guy. Not only will knowledge of the existence of the injection system aid our cause, but so will knowledge of his response to our sabotaging it. He's making the people pay for something that ought to come out of his pocket. I don't think they'll be happy to hear that, do you?"

"No, I guess not."

"Good. Speaking of which..." Jake stood up. "Come with me. I've figured out a good way for you to help the cause." He led her to the communications and sensor room. "This will be where you'll play your part from."

It took her a moment to catch on. "Oh, I get it. You want me to make pirate broadcasts. I secretly send attack signals to our friends on the planet so they can sabotage Maxis and his thugs?"

"No. I want you to help subvert Maxis' authority by making fun of him, and by pointing out the flaws in the system. Spread rumors. You're a teenager, you ought to be very good at that."

"Oh."

"Start figuring out to work everything. Don't send any messages right now. Wait for my orders, like always. Just play around and get the hang of everything."

"Hey, I already know how to use some of this."

"Figure it all out. Oh, and also figure out the identity cloaking equipment. After all, everyone knows your face and voice."

"Yeah, so?"

"We don't need any celebrity endorsements." Evvie shook her head. Jake sighed, then said, "If Maxis sees you, he might start looking for you. And then he might find us, and..."

"Oh."

"Right, oh. Once you get this figured out, we'll work on scripts."

"I can write my own material. I do it all the time. Well, most of the time. Oh, okay, some of the time. But I can write."

Jake paused for a moment to think. "Let me put it to you this way." He took a step closer to her. "I'll let you improvise, so long as you stick the main point of the script, okay?"

"Okay."

"Then get to it." He turned to leave.

"Wait."

"What?"

"Can't you show me...?"

"Manuals are on the shelf over there."

"Manuals? I have read, too? Geez, this is just like school."

"Think of it as continuing education. And that what you might learn may advance your career as a pop star. But if this is too much work for you, well, I'm sure you'll enjoy the video of this story when it comes out."

"Over there, huh? Well, a little reading won't kill me, right? And like you said, I'll learn some things the other stars don't know. Can only help me, right?"

Nine
Hip To Be A Rebel

The mine workers of Antioch Two knew theirs was a hard life. They were at their jobs from breakfast to dinner, with a "long" break for lunch and shorter breaks at midmorning and mid-afternoon. They weren't paid as such; in exchange for their labor they were given unlimited food, a place to live, unlimited access to cultural activities and material, and a free off-world retirement plan. Clothing was provided, but styles and variations were not. Slacking on the job was not tolerated. Advancement options were strictly limited. Parents could only have one child unless they managed to advance up the ladder or gain other recognition.

Still, most told themselves, their lives could be much worse. They could be forced to actually dig the minerals out of the planet.

In fact their "work" was not hard physical labor as such. Some workers had to operate the machines that did the real digging, but this mainly consisted of pushing keypads and moving joysticks. Others drove carts that carried the trailers into which the raw ore was dumped to a separation station. Some worked at the separation station, and a few more worked the system that transported the separated ore to the refinery. Days were long and duties repetitive, but danger was low and tiring effort was even more minimal. Work days were uneventful unless something went wrong, and things rarely went wrong.

Then one day, specifically a few days after the drug injection system was sabotaged, something did go wrong. The mining machinery came to an abrupt stop. Power levels in the equipment and vehicles suddenly dropped to zero. At first everyone assumed it was due to a failure in the power system, until they realized that the lights were still on and the life support system was still active.

The next strange thing to happen was that the intercom system came alive.

"Hey, there, citizens!" a perky voice called. "This is Edie Freedom, your voice of resistance. Say, all you in the mines. Did you know your labor brings in over one and a half million credits every year in profits to your planet? And guess where all those profits don't go? To you!

"But wait, it gets better. You're not supposed to be treated this way, but your boss is handing out creds to keep his suppliers looking the other way. Isn't that nice of Mister Maxis?

"Now, unpaid workers, here's some subversive music to give you time to think about these uncool arrangements."

The music that followed was not what Maxis would have allowed to be played over the planet's audiocast system. The norm were passive, nonvocal arrangements of pop standards. What did follow were classic rock tunes about rebellion, outlaw behavior, and goofing off. Almost a dozen songs played before the audio was switched off and the power was restored to the equipment.

***

That night Odin told Jake that he believed the Rosens were trying to get in touch with him. When asked why he believed that, Odin said, "They appear to be attempting to send out audio signals on various frequencies."

"Oh. Well, tell them to stop before they get intercepted." Jake paused for an instant. "Y'know, I really ought to send them something so that if they have to get in contact with us, they'd be able to."

"Wise thinking, Jake. I shall prepare an inventory of parts on hand, and remind you of the project in the morning."

"Thank you."

"In the meantime, the Rosens on screen."

The couple appeared on the bridge screen in front of Jake. "Were you the one who sent out that audiocast today?" Clarissa asked breathlessly.

"Who else would it be? The Galaxy's Top Forty?"

"Oh, right."

"What do we do now?" Daniel asked.

"Nothing." Jake smiled. "Let Maxis pull his hair out trying to figure out where the audio is coming from. He'll waste his guards' time and effort, and his credits, looking for the source."

"He won't trace it back to you?"

"No. Odin's gotten into his systems, spoofed the trail, and just generally made certain there's no way we can be found. But he and the other execs will go nuts searching for a secret transmitter, or a penetration into his software and hardware."

96

"Is there anything we should do?" Daniel asked again.

"No. Oh, you might warn everyone to expect Maxis to crack down on you when nothing turns up."

"Like what?"

"My guess is maybe eliminating breaks, or cutting your lunch hour down."

"Oh. Well, I suppose we can handle that."

"Just make certain word gets out as a rumor, not as your informed opinion."

"Right."

"Oh, and tomorrow, I'm going to work on something that you can use if you want to contact us."

"Great."

"Until then, sit tight. We're just getting this show started."

***

The next day during the main lunch for the workers there was another audio interruption in the routine.

"Edie Freedom here again," the perky, electronically-cloaked voice said. "I was just wondering how Sordius Maxis got a name like that. Aren't you wondering the same thing? Y'know, his initials are S and M. Maybe that has something to do with it?"

Bits of giggles broke out among the workers. At least one even spat out a bit of food onto his plate. The two human guards looking on didn't try to sober up the chortling crowd. They were too busy listening in themselves.

"Say, I don't mean to imply that ol' Max is a pervert. But, he does get all those creds from your labor. And he never goes on vacations, never throws big parties, and doesn't invest in more mines. Where do all those creds go? Here's some tunes to help you think."

This time the audio cut out after only three songs, but the damage had been done. An hour later Maxis called in his executives for an emergency meeting. Listening in through the bug, Jake could tell that the man in charge was white-hot with anger.

"I want these broadcasts stopped!" he screamed once the last executive was seated. "I don't care what it takes or how much its costs!"

"We still can't find the source," Thorne reported. "I had guards searching yesterday, last night, and this morning. Nothing! I went through our software, in case it came in through a data stream. There's been no tampering, no hacking, no trace of where these broadcasts are coming from."

"Well, they aren't coming in through magic, are they? Keep looking."

"What do we do in the meantime?" the young woman named Tina asked. "If something isn't done, the workers will think someone's getting away with making us look bad."

"End the midmorning and mid-afternoon breaks," Maxis answered. "We need the increased output. And if they complain, tell them we'll reinstate the breaks if they tell us who's behind these broadcasts. Now, get back to work."

As the meeting broke up and the audio faded to nothing, Jake shook his head. "What did I say? It's like Maxis is reading from a script."

He stood up. "Odin, where's Evvie?"

"I believe she's working on her next broadcast. In the comm room."

"Thanks." Jake left the bridge and went to the comm room. Sure enough, Evvie was looking over her lines and scanning a playlist. Jake felt some relief at the sight of her applying herself to the effort. *Maybe there's hope for her yet,* he thought.

She turned to him as he entered the room. "Hey, Jake. What'd ya think?"

"About?"

"My broadcast. That 'S and M' gag go over well?"

"Apparently so. Maxis has just revoked breaks for the workers. I'm surprised that you got the joke, though."

"Well, I had to look it up," she admitted. "The research made me fell kinda... nasty. I hope you're not going to make me tell more of those kinds of jokes. I don't want to get caught looking up that sort of stuff."

"I won't. I came here because I think we need to let the people know who's supporting 'Edie's' broadcasts."

"What do you mean?"

"Well, aside from the workers, who is Edie speaking for? What group?"

"Oh, you want to form a group?"

"Not yet. Just a name for the group to start with."

Evvie smiled. "I'm glad you're asking me, Jake. I've been doing some more research on rebellions and stuff. I'll bet I can come up with a great name."

"Well, I did have my own ideas. But if you'd like to give it a shot, go."

"Okay." She thought for a moment. "I suppose we have to get the planet's name into it, right?"

"Yes."

"Okay." She thought a bit more. "How about the Antioch Liberation Front?"

"A-L-F. Alf." Jake shook his head. "Too cutesy."

"Antioch Rebellion... Force."

"A-R-F. Arf. Extremely silly. Try again."

"Rebels for Antioch Freedom. R-A-F."

"Royal Air Force. Major name in Earth history."

"Oh. Yeah, might be too confusing when the video comes out. How about the Antioch Liberation Army?"

"A-L-A? Okay name, but the initials sound like a business firm or a lobbying group."

"Wait. How about the Antioch Liberation Group?"

"A-L-G?"

"Yeah. I mean, 'group' is lots nicer than 'army,' or 'command,' or 'force.' It doesn't spell anything. And it's group, and it's liberating Antioch Two, right?"

"It's still not very decisive."

"Yeah, but it's there, but not scary, y'know?"

Jake thought it over. *On the one hand, she does have a point. A threatening name would make it hard to get people involved. A 'group' doesn't have to do anything violent, whereas an 'army' or a 'force' almost has to. And you know, there's something perversely funny about a 'liberation group.' It almost qualifies as an oxymoron.*

And I'm certainly having to deal with morons, oxy and otherwise, around here.

He sighed. "Well, I can't think of any names that, as you said, aren't 'scary.' So A-L-G it is. Congratulations, Evvie. You've made another vital contribution to the cause of freedom. Now, get back to work on your next one."

***

The ALG's debut came three mornings later when the all the

99

planet's workers would have break. The minute after the break would have started every machine used for work on Antioch Two shut down, except of course for life support and the intercom, the latter coming to life within seconds.

"Hello again, everyone, Edie Freedom on the line once again. Say, did you know that by interstellar law, you're entitled to paid retirement? You're the one who's supposed to be in control of that retirement plan. But guess what? That's right, Maxis has his grubby fingers in that pie, too.

"When you get too old to work, he sends you to the retirement center he chooses. He pockets your pension, takes kickbacks from the center, and they keep collecting government benefits long after you pass on. Don't you just love that?

"By the way, this bit of exposure is brought to you by the Antioch Liberation Group. Dedicated to restoring your rights and your fair share. Now, here's some music to annoy the boss."

The broadcast was followed by three songs. When the last one ended, the machinery was powered back up. Naturally the broadcast was the talk of the planet for the rest of the day. Even more naturally, it led to a call from the Rosens to Jake.

"What's this Antioch Liberation Group?" Daniel asked.

"Should we organize?" Clarissa asked.

"No," Jake said, answering the latter question. "Continue to lie low. The object is to again get Maxis looking for something that doesn't exist."

"People are talking, Jake," Daniel said. "I think they need a forum."

"No, they don't. Not yet, anyway. In fact, we're going off the air for a week."

"Whatever for?"

Jake smiled. "To find out who's really interested, and who's just generally unhappy. I want you two, as quietly as possible, find out who really wants to commit to an effort to overthrow Maxis. Don't ask right out; steer a conversation in that direction. Be subtle. We'll let you know when we do another broadcast. The day before ask again. That should give you some idea of who's interested, and who's just discontented with their life. We want people from the first group, not the second."

"All right."

"Chin up, kids. These things take time. We'll be in touch. Take care, and remember the key word, 'subtle.'"

***

Sure enough, late the following week when the morning break should have happened there was another interruption and another broadcast from "Edie." This time the subject was the real estate deal Maxis' grandfather had made.

"Friends, you might not be too surprised to hear this, but Maxis' grandfather lied to his employers on how rich this world is. He bought this planet cheap, made a fortune, and passed down his corruption and ill-gotten gains to his son and his grandson. It was all completely illegal. I guess in the case of Sordius and his family, some behavior is inherited. Too bad it's criminal behavior.

"Now the ALG will bring you more music to undermine the unjust authorities. And to the oppressed and exploited workers, hey, have a great day!"

That night the Rosens again got in contact with Jake. They first presented their list of names to him. Then Daniel asked, "Can we organize now? I have some ideas on how we might hold meetings."

"I'm sure you do," Jake said. "You're wrong."

"How do you know what I was thinking?"

Because you always go with the obvious, Jake wanted to say. "Any attempt you make to hold secret meetings at an odd time will get found out. Now, as you said a while back, Sundays are your day for cultural activities, right? Including club meetings, true?"

"Yeah."

"Well, you're going to form a new club for this Sunday. The Twenty-First Century American Literature group. Official initials, T-F-C-A-L. Unofficial initials, ALG." He smiled and opened his hands in front of the screen. "There you are. You'll be meeting right in the open, where Maxis and his cronies would never think to look."

"Oh. Wow, that is clever."

"What if too many people start showing up?" Clarissa asked.

"Invitation only," Jake told her, "on recommendation of a trusted member. And we'll conduct background checks first."

"Do we just meet, then? No secret names, no disguises, nothing like that?"

Jake closed his eyes. *It would be amusing to see a meeting like that. But I have to take this seriously.* "No. The more it behaves like a normal club, the less attention it will draw to itself.

"Now, I want you two to get the club formed and meeting space secured. Odin found out that one of the school rooms is free. If you have any problems let us know. We can manipulate the data to get everything set. Since this will be a weekly club, getting a meeting spot will be tricky, but that'll be to our advantage. Once the meeting it set up, send out a normal notice to everyone on the list. We'll send an anonymous second message about what will really happen. And speaking of, we're sending you a meeting agenda. Don't deviate from it. Turn on that little contact device I gave you when the meeting starts. I'll be listening in, and I can talk if I have to."

Daniel nodded. "All right. We'll run the meeting, then?"

"Yes. I won't step in unless I have to. You two are now in charge of the Antioch Liberation Group."

"Great. We'll get started on our end right now."

"Stay in touch, and be careful. Out."

A moment after the image on the screen faded Odin said, "Jake, I do have one question about your plan?"

"Only one? I must be doing something right."

"Why a group on American literature of the Twenty-First Century? I was not aware that there was much literature from America, or anywhere else, at that time."

"Ah. That." Jake shrugged. "Well, compared with now, that time was virtual golden age of literature. Any older period, and we might actually get someone who's really interested in the topic, but not in revolution. And there aren't that many countries that start with 'A.'"

"There are colonies."

"True, but have they produced anything worth discussing week after week?"

"I see your point."

"And I do see yours, Odin. But I suspect Maxis' inner circle does not include any serious and learned literary scholars. In fact, I'd be willing to bet that 'scholar' is the last thing you'd call any of them. I think the ALG will be safe from any unsavory attention for awhile, Odin."

***

Jake was back in his chair on the bridge when the first meeting of the ALG began early the following Sunday afternoon. He allowed Evvie to sit next to him, but told her to keep silent during the meeting. "You aren't here to make suggestions," he said, "just to listen. If the meeting gets bogged down, I'll get it moving." Evvie agreed, and Jake instructed Daniel and Clarissa that things were ready on his end.

He heard Daniel stand up. "Thanks for coming, everyone. I'd like to welcome all of you to the kickoff meeting of the Antioch Liberation Group. I'm glad that you all support our ideals, and I hope this is the start of positive change for all of us, and for everyone else on our planet."

"Get on with it," Jake muttered.

"We all know each other, and because of security, we won't do any introductions. Instead, our format will be a greeting, followed by new business. If we get to a point where we have to take care of old business, we'll do that next, and then we'll wrap things up." There was a pause. "Yes?"

"What about new members?" a woman asked.

"That'd be new business, I think. Jake?"

"Get on with it," Jake answered slowly, "this is a revolution, not a social club."

"Oh, right. Well, let's start with why we need to take these steps. Clarissa?" Daniel sat down, and she stood up.

"Thanks," she said. "As you are all aware, we are being oppressed and exploited. Furthermore, we have proof that Maxis is denying us our share in the profits of our world's resources. Finally, as you'd heard through the 'Edie Freedom' audiocasts, Maxis has engaged and is engaging in illegal and corrupt practices."

Evvie tapped Jake's arm and smiled. He nodded, then put his right forefinger in front of his mouth.

"I think the oppression is cause enough," Clarissa continued. "But this corruption could be a serious problem down the road. People might assume that we support it, when in fact we don't. So if Maxis was caught and arrested in the future, and our rights were restored, the markets might not want to buy what we mine, or they might want to but at a lower price."

"We need to take action not only for us," Daniel said, "but for the future prosperity of our world."

"How do we go about this?" a man asked.

"We have a plan of action from our new friend, Jake," Clarissa answered. "He's agreed to help us oust Maxis, in return for a share of our gross profits. I hope that's okay with everyone?"

"As long it all works out," another man said. Quiet laughter filled the room.

"Right. Well, I'll let Daniel outline the action plan." She sat down and he stood up again.

"Okay, well, first off, we need to have a work stoppage when we would have had our regular break. We'd like to do this Wednesday morning. I think that gives us enough time to spread the word, but not enough time for it to be interfered with. Yes?"

"What's the purpose of this work stoppage?" another man asked.

"The stoppage has two goals. First is to show that we have support. So it's important that everyone spread the word about it. Second, this would be the first act to protest how we're treated."

"Weren't the breaks taken away because of your broadcasts?"

"Actually, they aren't *ours*, per se. They originate from a secret site. But to answer your question, no. Our workload was increased so that the executives can pay for new equipment and not have to dip into what they're making. Taking away the breaks was a major part of that increase."

"How do you know that?"

"We..."

"Have inside information," Jake said. "The Rosens wouldn't be carrying this out without knowing the truth of what's going on."

"Very kind of you," Odin told Jake in a low tone.

"That's right," Daniel said. "In fact, I think over time we'll release information to all of you that will help you convince others that what we're doing is right and just.

"Okay, well, we do this work stoppage on Wednesday morning. We'll see how we do, but I'd like to do more next week, so make sure you get the word out. Oh, and don't forget, we don't want to get shut down. Don't tell any of the forepersons, guards, and definitely don't tell the executives.

"Now, once we're on our feet and can get a good turnout, we should stage a protest march or rally down the road. We might also think about circulating a petition for our rights, for our share of profits, and so on. Over this week, if any of you get any ideas, speak up at next week's meeting. I think if we all pull together, we can be a force for real positive change.

"Are there any more questions? No? Okay, then. This has been a good first meeting. Let's pull for a good showing at the work stoppage Wednesday morning. If that's it, we're adjourned. We'll meet again next Sunday to discus things. We'll let you know where and what time by Friday. Thanks for coming out."

Jake shut off the audio as the sounds of a meeting ending rose. An instant later he sighed and rolled his eyes. "Did he just say 'thanks for coming out?'"

"He did," Odin said.

"Would you call that an unintentional choice of words or a clueless goodbye?"

"I believe I will leave the cynicism to you."

"Oh, but I have so much. Can't I share?"

***

The next Sunday the ALG met in a different classroom at a slightly later time. The attendees from the first meeting were all there, and were joined by two new members. Once again Daniel took the part of meeting leader and facilitator.

"We'll start with old business, namely the work stoppage," he began. "I think we should give ourselves a hand. About ninety percent of the workers stopped on Wednesday, and we managed to keep the stoppage going for a full ten minutes. Great job!" The sound of clapping filled the room.

"I think we should try for three stoppages this coming week: another Wednesday morning, one Thursday afternoon, and one Friday morning. If we can get strong responses all three days, that'll go a long way towards our goal. That leads us to new business. First, Clarissa has a report on the possibility of a petition drive." He sat down and she stood up.

"Thanks. I've found a clause in our standard work contract that does grant us the right to appeal unjust actions on the part of foremen to the executive council. I think this is our method of approach on this topic. We need a grievance as the subject of our petition. It has to be something that they are doing to us, but also something that they can't solve on their own. Any suggestions?"

"How about restoration of the break periods?" one man asked.

"That's close, but it's too minor a grievance. We need something major."

"Profit-sharing?" another asked.

"The executives have control of that, not the forepersons."

"The child policy?"

"Same."

"Shift safety?"

"Unfortunately, that's not a problem right now."

"I say go with the break periods," Jake said.

"Why's that?"

"It might be minor, but it's an opening. You'll force the executives to either reject you out of hand or give in to the petition. If they turn you down, that's a propaganda victory, proof that they don't care about the ordinary worker. If they grant the petition, you've asserted some real power. You can start bombarding them with petitions for major grievances like profit-sharing and such."

"I have a question," a woman said. "How do we present this petition? I mean, if one of us shows up with it, won't the executives know who we are, what we're up to?"

"Not if it's an anonymous posting," Jake answered. "You get the signatures. When you think you can't get any more, send it to me. I have a way of sending it out to everyone without it being traced back to any one person. The petition becomes an open secret. There are all these names supporting it, but no one signee claims credit for being behind it. Get enough names, and there are simply too many people for the executives to retaliate against."

"Either they deal with it or they ignore it," Clarissa said. "But they can't punish us for it. Thanks, Jake. If there's nothing else, then, I guess I'm done." She sat down.

Daniel stood up again. "Okay. Clarissa, you draft the petition. We'll figure out a way to get it around. If there's no other discussion? Let's call for a vote. All in favor of the petition plan, raise your right hand. Opposed, same sign. Great. I think we'll try to get that going this week.

"Next on the agenda is a protest march. I'd like to form a committee to explore a route, a theme, and to find a time to carry one out."

"When would this committee meet?" another woman asked.

"We'll do our business through Jake's secure system. I'll let you know the details once you're in. Any volunteers? Carol? Good. Frank, okay. Chris? Okay, I think that'll do. I'll be on it too, if that's okay. I don't think we need to vote on this. Anyone disagree? No? Great.

"Well, I think that's it for new business. Remember, these meetings are being held in secret. Don't spread the word about them. If someone asks, or if you overhear that someone's interested, send their name to us. We need to make sure Maxis and his cronies don't break us up. Okay, well, we're making progress. We'll see you next Sunday. We are adjourned."

***

Over the week that followed the second meeting things moved quickly. The first two work stoppages went off without hitches, each lasting ten minutes. The petition was electronically signed by a fourth of the planet's workers in four days. As the Friday morning stoppage occurred the petition was anonymously circulated. Maxis and his executives couldn't help but notice that things were rapidly heading downhill. He brought them together that afternoon to figure out how to deal with the growing situation. And like every previous executive meeting, Jake and Odin were listening to every word.

"There's no way we can crack down on this petition," Thorne told them. "There's just too many workers, and no single source."

"Well, we can't accept it," Maxis replied. "We give in on this, and pretty soon those idiots will be asking us for everything."

"What should we do about these stoppages?" an executive asked. "They're defeating the purpose of the break cutback."

"We can't force people to work if they don't want to," Thorne said.

"Why not?"

"How do we force them to work that doesn't involve physical harm? It's not like we have an unemployed population sitting around waiting to take their place."

"We could bring in unemployed from other worlds."

"And deal with their unemployment agencies and labor departments?"

"Oh."

"Face it, we have no leverage. We can't harm them and risk sending them to the sickbay, and we don't have any real benefits that we can cut."

"Benefits," Maxis said softly. "Benefits. Benefits..."

"Sir?"

"I have it," he said a moment later. "I've got a clever plan that will undermine those malcontents. We'll allow the workers to form a union. Thorne, you set it up for the cafeteria sometime on Sunday. Make sure word gets out, too."

"How does that help?"

"Simple. We'll let them form this union to negotiate this break thing. Only when they come to negotiate, we'll offer them lousy terms. No break restoration for six months."

"They'll refuse."

"No. Either they accept, or we refuse to ever restore the break period. And we tell them that any other negotiations will be at our discretion, or we make half of Sunday a work day. That should shut them up."

"That is a pretty clever plan, sir," Thorne said.

"No, it isn't," Jake said. He let out a laugh. "Now, how to phrase it? Yes." He remembered a favorite video from his youth, "Black Adder." He took on the voice of the main character, his becoming at once English, intelligent, smug, and just a bit mean. "Maxis wouldn't know a clever plan if it painted itself purple and danced through the corridors singing, 'Clever plans are here again.'" Returning to his normal voice, he said, "Odin, monitor the rest of the meeting. I think I'll give the Rosens a call."

***

The following Sunday evening Thorne went to see Maxis in his quarters. His superior was surprised by the visit, and by the discouraged look on his face. "Come in, come in. What's wrong?"

Thorne sat down across from Maxis. "That union thing was a flop."

"No!"

"Yes."

"Didn't anyone show up?"

Thorne laughed bitterly. "Oh, sure. Five workers came in five minutes after the meeting was supposed to start."

"Five?"

"Yeah, five. And these five were the absolute dregs, I gotta tell you. The low end of the mining operation. And do you know why they bothered to show up?"

"No, why?"

Thorne shook his head. "They thought this union would be their chance to climb up out of the dirt. They all said they wanted to be in charge of the union so everyone else would look up to them. They didn't care about negotiations. They just wanted to get ahead."

"So why didn't anyone else show up? This was a good plan."

"I dunno. Maybe they didn't trust me. I mean, even if I didn't say so, everyone knew I was trying to get it organized. Maybe that spooked them."

"So we try again. Only we get some workers to organize it."

"Who? The proles that showed up today? Who do we find that won't keep his or her mouth shut? Because if whoever we get starts blabbing, what happened today happens again."

"Damn! So what do we do?"

"I say we give in on this break thing and hope that shuts them up for awhile. Maybe Tina can juggle the books a bit so profits don't get eaten up as much. I'll see if I can figure out how we can put this thing down before it gets out of hand."

"You do that. We've got a good thing going here. If it goes to Hell, it's gonna be everyone for himself."

***

The next morning Jake and Evvie discussed the rebellion's first collective success. At one point she asked him about how he'd managed to undermine Maxis' plan. "I mean, great for our side and all," she said, "and that was real smooth, getting those guys to dress like they did and say what they said."

"Is there a point somewhere?"

"Well, I was just wondering if you thought shooting down Maxis like that was kinda mean?"

"Of course it was mean. He is the enemy, Evvie."

"I know, I know."

"And don't think for a moment that he wouldn't try something just like that to beat us. Revolutions aren't pretty, and there can be only one winner. You have to break eggs to make an omelet, y'know."

"Yeah. What's an omelet?"

Ten
Blows To The Head

"Start tapping into the feeds, Odin," Jake said. He sat down on the couch on the lower bridge. The big screen in front of him came to life with an image of the cafeteria in the main dome. Smaller images from other security cameras focused on the same room appeared in boxes at the top of the screen.

Evvie entered the room an instant later carrying a medium-sized bowl. She sat down on the couch, keeping some space between her and Jake.

Jake looked at her, then at the bowl. It was filled with what appeared to be chocolate-covered popcorn. "This isn't a movie, y'know," he said to her, still looking at the bowl.

"Hey, I've been on strict regimen on the tour. I haven't had this in over a year."

Jake frowned for a moment. On the one hand, he was pleased that she actually indulging in real teenaged behavior. On the other, he was displeased that this was the time for such behavior. He opted to go with the latter feeling and said, "This is work, Evvie, not entertainment."

"I know. But it's gonna be boring, and I'll fall asleep if I don't have something to eat while I watch. I'll share, if you want some."

"No thanks. Just eat quietly." Jake's attention returned to the screen.

The image in front of them showed a gathering of people in the cafeteria. The Rosens were in the center of the assembly, but not giving orders. They were leaving that duty to the "committee" that had organized the pending march. Once the committee was certain no one else was going to show up, they began handing out signs with slogans on them.

"I did those," Evvie told Jake.

"Did what?"

"Those signs."

Jake looked. The signs demanded restoration of breaks, reduction of work periods, and better treatment overall. They appeared to be lacking in obvious teenage touches like cute lettering and frivolous colors. "You designed and printed those yourself? I'm impressed."

"Well, Odin helped with the production."

And no doubt restrained your inclinations, Jake thought. He mouthed "Thank you" to the upper deck of the bridge.

Once the dozen or so signs were distributed among the crowd, they formed into three lines. At a nod from one of the committee members, the lines began to move through the cafeteria towards one of the corridors. The leaders of the march began to chant, "Hey hey, ho ho, unfair treatment's got to go." A moment later the rest of the marchers picked up on the chant.

"Where are the guards and the bots?" Evvie asked.

"Odin?"

"The guardbots are withdrawn from areas once an area has ceased being occupied," the computer said. "No doubt after tonight that policy will be reviewed."

"And the guards?"

"Currently trying to obtain orders."

"Keep us informed," Jake instructed.

The marchers entered the corridor that led to the quarters of the various foremen. The dome's corridors generally radiated out from a central point, then connected these spokes with an outer rim corridor. It was a standard feature of such domes that allowed residents to get anywhere on a level without having to worry about their main access corridor being blocked. But in this instance, it allowed the marchers to head past those quarters and return to the cafeteria without having to turn around and retrace their steps.

Odin arranged the view on the screen so that the front of the march was the large view. The smaller images were side and back views. As the marchers approached the end of the corridor he replaced one of the side views to an image of the cafeteria. It showed a half-dozen guards assembled around one of the executives. Once the guards were in place the executive led them along the route the marchers had taken.

"Is this going to get nasty?" Evvie asked.

"I doubt it," Jake said.

"They are armed, y'know."

"But they haven't drawn their blasters. As long as the marchers don't pick a fight, nothing's going to happen."

As it was, the guards had to jog to catch up with the protest march, which had now turned into the rim corridor. When they reached that spot the executive spoke into a wrist communicator, asking for further instructions. He held the wristcomm to his ear; Jake wondered if this was because whoever was giving the orders wasn't Maxis, and hadn't bothered to tell him what was going on. The executive nodded, then motioned for the guard to continue the pursuit.

It wasn't long before word of the guard's trailing of the march spread among the protesters. Nervousness tinged with fear dashed through the ranks until Clarissa spoke up. "Just keep doing like we planned," she said loud enough so she could be heard. "Don't look back, and don't speak to the guards."

The marchers turned at the next corridor, continued past some classrooms, and reentered the cafeteria. They switched from being in a line to forming a rough circle. They continued chanting as the guards followed them into the room.

The executive nodded to the guards. Three lined up on his left, and three did so on his right. They put their hands on their sidearms. "Stop this nonsense and return to your quarters," he yelled.

The protesters went silent for an instant. Then on a cue from their leaders, they cheered. The sign holders waved their signs in the air. They waved to the guards and the executive, and promptly dispersed.

"What was that all about?" Evvie asked.

Jake smiled. "A little moral victory."

"Huh?"

"That exec, and whoever's giving him his orders, probably assumed that the protesters wouldn't leave unless threatened, or that they'd have to use force to break it up. The cheer and the waves are to make it clear this was a peaceful protest. That'll make any crackdown on the workers look bad, an overreaction to people peacefully demanding their rights."

"And that'll make Maxis and his posse what? Confused? Scared?"

"Something like that."

"Oh. I guess I'm getting the hang of this revolution thing," she said proudly.

"I doubt that," Jake muttered.

112

***

The next morning Jake was back on the upper bridge. He was partly plotting strategy, and partly waiting for Maxis to assemble his executives. Jake wanted to know how they'd react to the march so as to tailor the response. He was busy going over his options when Odin interrupted his train of thought.

"Jake, I think you should speak to Miss Martini."

"Why?"

"I believe she's attempting to make a contribution to this effort."

"Good. A little hard work might be just what she needs."

"I do not think you, or anyone else, would appreciate this contribution. In fact, it might be vital that you stop her."

"Is she annoying you, Odin?"

"She is accessing my time and resources in a method that I believe would make you upset with both of us."

Jake wondered if he was detecting desperation in Odin's voice. "All right, I'll talk to her. Where is she?"

"In her quarters."

Jake rose from his seat and strode to her room. He tapped the door chime keypad. Evvie yelled "Come in," and the door opened. He found her sitting on her bed, an open notebook of paper perched on her lap and a pen in her right hand.

I don't like the looks of this.

"What are you up to, Evvie?"

She grinned. "I'm writing a song."

"This is hardly the time..."

"No, no, a song for the revolution."

"Excuse me?"

"Y'know, a song to inspire the people. A theme song, if you like."

"I don't like."

"Why not?"

"Well, for one thing, there isn't going be any news on this until it's over."

"I know. This is just for the people down there. And maybe for the drama."

"I doubt they need an anthem, Evvie."

"Hey, you do your thing, and I'll do mine."

"I thought you didn't write your own material."

"Well, I helped on my last two singles. And I do wanna write my own stuff."

"Let me see."

"I don't know..."

"Let me see," Jake repeated, louder and slower.

Evvie sighed and handed him her notebook. He gasped when he read the first two lines: "Freedom is worth fighting for,/ Abuse ain't worth dying for."

"What?"

"This beginning."

"What's wrong with my beginning?"

"For one thing, it's a subtle as a brick through a window. I mean, this is a horrible opening to a song. And at any rate, we are not a bunch of cammoflage-clad guerillas in the mountains of Podunkistan battling against the army of El Supremo the Dictator. This is a peaceful effort to remove a corrupt boss."

Jake shook his head and continued reading. After suffering through the rest of the first stanza, he came to the rap-flavored chorus. It contained the phrase, *"Can't you see, we gotta be free/ It's all about justice and liberty."*

"This chorus is pretty lousy for a rap," he said. "It's also too obvious by a long shot. I mean, it's not as if Maxis is openly against freedom and liberty. Again, this is not about dictatorship so much as it's about corrupt and greedy management."

"Well, skip to the end. Maybe you'll like that."

He exhaled, but soldiered on at his pace. He struggled through a bad second stanza, a worse third, an oddly-noted dance interlude, then came to the "grand finale." It consisted of the following four lines: *"We all gotta have our rights/ We all gotta speak the truth/ You can't suppress the dreams of age/ You can't suppress the hopes of youth."* Jake found himself coughing after reading those lines, almost as if he was allergic to them.

"Now what?"

"Well, for starters, I now see why you don't write your own material, Evvie. Those last four lines are just ridiculous! This 'dreams of age' thing makes absolutely no sense. The 'hope of youth' sounds juvenile. You're almost skirting the edge of that old standard, 'You gotta fight for the right to party.'

"Overall, this song veers wildly between being optimistic and being downbeat. It feels like the rhythm is off. The rhyming patterns don't fit. It looks like it's trying way too hard to be an anthem. I hate to say this, Evvie, because I have to admit that you are a nice person and a good singer, but this is a terrible song. Calling this a first draft is an insult to every bad first draft of a song ever written.

"Look, just do as I tell you to. If you have an idea for a contribution, ask me first. As much as you get on my nerves, I do appreciate your help, Evvie. But if you insist on trying to help with stuff like this song, you'll force me to edge you out of this. You don't want to miss out on this opportunity, do you?"

"No."

"Of course not. So just stick with the plan. And if you're nice, I might even help you become a better songwriter." He handed the notebook back to her.

"I don't know if I want your help if you're gonna be mean."

"No one likes constructive criticism until it proves correct."

"Jake, the meeting is getting underway," Odin said.

"Good. C'mon, Evvie. Let's see what Maxis is going to do now."

"Awright." She followed him out of her room and back onto the bridge. They took their seats on the upper level and waited for Odin to begin the audio feed from the bug in the meeting room.

"All right, let's look at it," Maxis ordered. Apparently the first thing the executives were going to do was watch the footage of the march. The sounds of the march were low. Occasionally there would come over it a "hmph," a murmur, or a whisper.

"How long is this gonna take?" Evvie asked.

"Shut up and listen," Jake replied.

At length the video of the march reached the point where Clarissa urged calm when the guards showed up. Someone close to the bug shifted in his seat. "Stop!" Maxis ordered. "Can you get a close-up on that woman?"

"I'll try." Odin's real-time transcript identified the speaker as Morton, the head of Maxis' guard force.

"I don't like this," Jake said. He crossed his arms over his chest.

"That's Clarissa!" Maxis yelled a moment later.

"Who?" Thorne asked.

"Y'know, that chick that dumped me in high school for what's his name, Danny Rosen."

"That's her?"

"Look at her."

"Yeah, I guess you're right."

"Morton?"

"Just a moment, sir. Uh, it appears to be a Clarissa Rosen, of..."

"I knew it," Maxis snapped, cutting Morton off.

"Uh, what should we do, sir? Pick her and her husband up?"

"Hang on. Let me think."

Jake took his right hand from his chest and covered his face with it. "Odin, did either of the Rosens mention a prior relationship with Maxis at any point in our past converstaions?"

"They did not."

"Did you come across any evidence of a such a prior relationship?"

"I did not."

"Swell. Just swell."

"What's the matter?" Evvie asked.

Jake was about to reply when he heard Maxis say "Okay." He opened his hand and tilted his head to listen.

"Bring Clarissa in after dinner. Just her, got it? You question her for as long as you can. She probably won't talk. Now, don't do anything to her. If she doesn't talk right off, wait half an hour. Leave her alone. Start up again. Keep that up till, say, midnight. Let her sleep a few hours, then try again. If she still doesn't talk, let her go back to sleep. I'll talk to her first thing tomorrow morning."

"And if she still won't talk about all this?" Thorne asked.

"Then we'll bring in that weasel husband of hers and threaten him. That should get her to tell us who's trying to screw things up around here."

"What are we going to do with them once we find them?"

"Well, we'll just have to make a few examples, show those proles what happens when they get out of line. We'll figure that out once we know who are the troublemakers, and who they've pressured into going along with them. Now, keep this quiet until tonight. Blabbermouths get demoted, got it? Good. Get back to work."

"Cut it," Jake said.

"We're gonna warn 'em, right?" Evvie asked.

"No."

She looked indignant. "Well, why not?"

"First off, how are we going to warn them? They're both working. Second, if we do warn them, what could they do? It's not like there's places to hide, or an outgoing ship at the spaceport they can catch. And finally, if we warn them and they do anything, Maxis will start wondering how they found out. Maybe he starts poking around for bugs. If he finds the one in the meeting room, he'll probably start looking for who planted it. It won't take his goons very long to find us if they really look."

"So what are we gonna do?"

"'We' aren't going to do anything. You will carry on with your broadcast. And no improvised warnings, either. I will think up some way to deal with this situation, and I will resolve it."

She glared at him for a moment, then lowered her head and shoulders. "If you say so." She turned and left the bridge.

Jake leaned back in his chair for a minute to think. "Odin, could you forge a local data file? Make it appear authentic?"

"Yes."

"How about a security video?"

"I can delete sections and insert new ones. I cannot reliably create a new video for insertion, especially if it involves human interactions. There are too many variables that could undermine my effort."

"Oh. Wait. We've got the holoroom. And video equipment."

"That would be a far more successful approach."

"Right. Get to work on scanning that control room. I'll do some tinkering, compose an outline, and prep a mechabug."

***

Clarissa jerked awake when Morton returned. She glanced around the room to see what time it was. A readout on one of the screens read "11:30." She tried to focus her mind on the task at hand. She was still in a chair, her wrists still bound, and she was still in security control under some sort of arrest.

"You're awake," Morton said. He smiled. "Good. I thought you were going to think about what I said."

Clarissa stared at him. She wanted to say something witty to him, but nothing came immediately to her. She decided instead to keep quiet.

"Now, I can have you back in your quarters right now if you just cooperate. Maybe the boss'll be nice and let you and Danny stay together. But you gotta tell me what's going on. Who's trying to mess things up, huh?"

"Your boss is," she replied.

He shook his head. "Now, we both know that's not... Hey!" He turned around, apparently looking for something. Just as he seemed to find whatever it was, his body relaxed. He closed his eyes and fell to the floor. Seconds later Jake materialized next to the guard.

"I knew you'd find out," she told him.

"About what, precisely?"

Her mind was still a little foggy. "What do you mean?"

"Your relationship with Maxis."

"I didn't have a relationship..." Her train of thought slammed on it brakes. "Oh, no. That's how he knew it was me."

"Would mind letting me in on this part of your past?"

"Um, could you untie me first?"

"No."

She frowned, then sighed. "Okay, Jake. It was nothing, really. When we were seniors he had a crush on me. He and I went out on a couple dates. I thought he was a creep. The next guy I went out with was Dan, and we've been together ever since. Now will you untie me? My arms are falling asleep."

He nodded, bent down, and freed her. He took a bracelet off his left wrist and handed it to her as she stood up. "Put this on."

She nodded towards Morton. "What about him?"

"He'll be sleeping all night."

She put the bracelet on. He spoke into his, and a few seconds later they were in the teleport room of his ship. "You can't hide me up here," she said.

"We're not going to hide you." He took off his bracelet, then hers.

"Then what are you up to?"

He smiled. "Time for the first episode of 'Antioch Two's Goofiest Home Videos.'" He waved to the doorway. "You're going to be the star, and I'll be Morton. C'mon."

"I hope you know what you're doing."

"I hope there isn't anything else about you and Maxis that you haven't told me."

***

The next morning Jake and Evvie were back on the upper level

Expert Assistance

of the bridge listening in on another executive meeting. They could tell that the atmosphere in the room was tense from shrill tone that had crept into Maxis voice.

"This morning when I went in to question Clarissa, I found this in the security log. You'll notice this confession on your screens. Read it."

"What does it say?" Evvie asked.

"Seems Clarissa admitted to stirring things up," Jake answered, "only it wasn't her idea."

"Whose idea was it?"

"Anyone notice my name as the instigator of this?" Maxis yelled.

"It... it has to be a forgery," Thorne said.

"You think so? Show them."

"Yes, sir," Morton said.

Jake and Evvie heard the audio of what seemed to be a recording made by a security camera. The audio was of Clarissa verbally stating her confession, the transcript of which had been on the executives' screens. Occasionally Morton would ask her a question or request a clarification. A third of the way through the recording the audio cut out.

"The date stamp has this being made from 11:30 to ten past midnight," Morton said. "The only problem is that right around 11:30 I was knocked out by a mechabug that injected me with some kind of sleep inducer. I was out all night."

"So it's a fake," one of the executives said.

"Of course it is," Maxis snapped.

"You think one of us did that?"

"Only Mister Maxis and Mister Thorne could have altered this data," Morton said.

The sound of a chair being pushed back came through the bug. "Hold on one minute!" Thorne's voice shook with rage. "It seems pretty clear to me that our systems have been compromised. I have nothing to gain from this forgery."

"Maybe not," Maxis countered, "but unless you can find out who compromised our systems, I have to conclude that you were behind this."

"And you..." Thorne took in a very loud breath. "Whoever had penetrated our system has done a pretty good job so far. They've got us yelling at each other over this bogus confession. I strongly suggest that we make a real effort to locate these crackers and stop them before they do more serious damage to us."

"Um, sir," the woman executive called Tina said, "I believe Mister Thorne is right. Somebody's playing with us. They might even be behind those troublesome workers and their march."

"I haven't found any evidence of tampering," Morton said.

"Just because you haven't found it doesn't mean it isn't there."

"This arguing is getting us nowhere," a second male executive said. "I think we should focus on the situation." There was an instant of silence, followed by the sounds of people sitting down. "Okay. First on the task list: what do we do about this Rosen woman? Do we bring her in again?"

"And have a repeat of last night?" Thorne asked.

"Do we discipline her?"

"For what?"

"Undermining my... our authority," Maxis said.

"Technically, she hasn't," Thorne told the others, "and if she has, what do we do about it? We don't have prison facilities. We don't even have a holding cell."

"We confine her to her quarters."

"And pretty soon lots of workers are gonna act up to get that punishment. We can't dock her pay or take away privileges. About all we can do is speed up our increase in schedules on the workforce. Once we've maximized that option that goes off the table."

"So what do you suggest?"

"Ease up on everyone except those workers that took part in the march."

"I don't like the sound of that," Jake said to Evvie.

"Why not?"

"It pits our friends against the other workers."

"I don't think that's a valid strategy," the second executive said after a moment's quiet. "I could radicalize those that get the increased workload, and that brings us back the dilemma of dealing with the Rosen woman, only on a larger scale."

Jake blew out a relieved breath. "Good point, there, buddy."

"Then, if there's no acceptable options," Thorne said, "I say we do nothing. If we can't do anything that makes the situation worse or makes us look bad, then the best thing we can do is nothing."

"We aren't going to do nothing." Maxis firmly put a hand on the meeting room table. "You are going to look for this cracker. Morton, make sure no more marches take place. The rest of you, send word down to your people that this sort of unrest will not be tolerated, and can lead to harsh measures. That's all."

Everyone rose from their seats. "Thorne, a moment." Once the others had left the room Maxis spoke to his right-hand man in a distinctly level tone. "Is there anything you want to tell me?"

Thorne's tone matched his boss. "Sordius, I'm not up to anything."

"You know I got you your position."

"And I'm grateful."

"So find this system cracker, or I'll have to do something."

"I am still your friend, but I won't take the blame for things I haven't done."

There were several moments of silence. They were ended by the sound of one man slapping the other's shoulders. "Do your job, then. Be my friend."

"Sure."

Maxis patted Thorne's shoulder again, and the two left the room. Odin switched off the audio from the bug.

"I think we have a winner," Jake said with some glee.

"A winner?" Evvie asked.

"Thorne."

"What's he won?"

"A conscience. Get back to work, Evvie. Odin, pull up the data on how Maxis' family got control of this world. I think it's time we shared this with more than just our friends in the ALG."

***

Jake knew that owning a teleporter carried with it certain ethics. They weren't rules as such, since his was the only private non-passenger starship so equipped, and he wasn't working for any government that might have its own regulations. But there were some things that he ordinarily wouldn't do. The first item on that list was teleporting into people's rooms without an invitation.

On the other hand, every job was different and would have their own set of rules and priorities. In this particular case, the priority was breaking down Thorne's loyalty to Maxis and getting him on the side of the revolution. While he could have Odin send down files, Jake knew there was a chance that Thorne wouldn't see them right away, much less draw the "right" conclusions. He could have sent a message, but despite their penetration there was still the possibility of the message being traced. There was no other way to open a dialog except to teleport into Thorne's room and talk to him.

To that end Jake considered wearing some sort of mask, another type of disguise, or something to alter his natural voice. He found three reasons not to. The first was that if Thorne wanted to discover Jake's identity he could do a scan, search a database, and learn it; a disguise wouldn't hide his identity for long. Second, Thorne might not be willing to trust someone who hid his face from him, and trust was important. The third reason was that it was the sort of dumb cliché' that the Rosens or Evvie might resort to if they were carrying this mission out.

Not that Jake was entirely trusting of Thorne; after all, he was on the wrong side of the revolution right at the moment. Jake made certain to arm himself before he teleported down. Nothing lethal, of course, but just enough to convince Thorne that funny business would not be tolerated.

Jake went down about an hour after the standard time that everyone on Antioch Two was supposed to go to sleep. Sure enough, there was Thorne, alone in his bed snoozing away. He waited for Odin to raise the light level in the room to medium-low before getting closer to the other man.

As the lights came up Jake got his first good look at Thorne. The man was tall, sturdily-built, and handsome, a complete opposite of the picture of a corporate flunky. However, two items did suggest to Jake that Thorne's life was that of an underling. First was the obvious fact that this stud was sleeping alone; no way that could happen unless his social life was a threat to his boss. Second was that even asleep Thorne had a concerned expression on his face. Jake knew that worry could only creep up during sleep on people who had no control over their lives.

In short, he thought, *Thorne really is the perfect choice for this approach.*

Jake approached the bed slowly and quietly as soon as the room had brightened a little. Once beside the bed he drew his stunner and poked it in Thorne's ear. "Wake up!" he shouted.

Thorne practically leapt out of bed. "What?"

Jake stepped back and smiled. "Hello." He pointed the weapon at Thorne. "Please don't call out."

Thorne rubbed his eyes. "You're not one of the guards. Who are you?"

"I heard you were looking for me, so I thought I'd take the initiative."

"Looking for you?" Thorne took a few moments to think. "You're the one who's broken into our systems?"

"More or less."

"Wait. How did you know we're looking for you?"

"Oh, I think you can figure that one out without my help."

Thorne sighed. "A bug." He sat up. "What is it you want?"

"Whoa!" In sitting up Thorne threw off his blanket, revealing that he slept in the least amount of underwear a man could. Jake put his left hand over his face. "That's a little too much personal data for me, buddy. Put that blanket back on you, or put on some pants."

"You're the intruder."

"Yeah, but not that kind of intruder."

Thorne gathered up the blanket and covered his lower half with it. "Happy?"

Jake dropped his left hand. "Thanks."

"Now, what the Hell do you want?"

"Well, as I said, I overheard that you're looking for me. I thought I'd come to you and let you know one reason why I'm up to what I'm up to."

"Okay, pal, enlighten me."

"Well, you do know how Maxis' granddad got ahold of this planet, don't you?"

"Sure. He bought it cheap from some corporation. Once he investigated Antioch Two he discovered what he'd found."

Jake let out a laugh and shook his head. "And they say we live in a cynical age. Gosh, that naiveté is, oh, I don't know, just so precious."

"What?"

"Mister Thorne, you've been had. You and everyone else on this rockball. Morgan Maxi was a planetary surveyor who lied to his employers about this planet. He told them it was a worthless place about to be teeming with life, instead of a dead chunk of rock and water containing several generations worth of loot. He and his son bought it cheap, and the family's been milking their boon for all it's worth ever since."

"I don't believe you."

"I thought you'd say that, so I took the trouble of having some files planted on your personal database."

"What files?"

"Maxi's report to his employers. His employment record. The real purchase agreement. Oh, I also put in a few interesting news pieces on Grandpa Maxi. Seems that if he hadn't made this world his private refuge, he'd have gone to court on a few worlds."

Thorne glanced away from Jake for a moment, then looked back at him. "Why tell me this? Why not go to the Earth authorities?"

"Legal loopholes, and the terms of my employment. Besides, you've struck me as a pretty smart guy. Take this morning's meeting. You were spot on when you suggested that the executives do nothing. Guys like you either know the score, or can figure it out.

"I think you'd agree with me that things are pretty crappy for the workers around here. Once you look over all that data, you'll see that you and the other executives aren't doing as well as you should, either. The only people ahead in this game are Sordius and the suits off-world that he's paying off."

Thorne glanced away again. "What if I tell Sordius about you?"

"There are no security cams in here. What proof do you have that I was even here? That data?" Jake shook his head. "Copies of all that data are sitting in very secure files that only Sordius has access to. You can find it off-world if you look, but I imagine he'll wonder why you have it. Did you break into his database? Are you trying to dig up dirt on him and his family? What would it be doing there, hm?

"No, I think telling him is a bad idea. In fact, I'd erase those files once you finish looking at them."

"Maybe I'll erase them before."

"Oh, I made certain you can't remove them until you open them, and once opened they won't close for a few minutes. I didn't want us going through the hassle of finding all that and handing it to you, only do have you junk it without even a peek at it."

"Okay, pal, say I do take a look. What am I supposed to do? Join you in your little resistance movement?"

Jake shook his head. "Nah. If I were you, I'd let that data percolate. Combine it with what you know about operations.

124

Consider the implications if certain things were told to certain authorities.

"Well, I think that's all for now. I don't know about you, but I've got a busy day tomorrow. We'll talk again soon." With that, Jake allowed Odin to teleport him out of Thorne's room, leaving the other man to ponder what he's said. Jake was fairly confident that the man would not get as good a night's sleep as he would.

**

A few days later another protest march was to be held. This one was to specifically call for reduced hours, profit-sharing, and better contacts with off-worlders. Once again Jake and Evvie sat on the upper level of the bridge to monitor the action.

This time, though, there were a few things different. The first was that Jake sent down to the Rosens earpieces for the clandestine comm unit he'd sent them previously. Jake was worried that this time around the marchers might run into more serious trouble. He didn't want them to respond to any situation unwisely. He gave the Rosens the earpieces and told them, "Do exactly as I tell you, or you're on your own."

Jake was proved right before the march began, for unlike last time guards and guardbots appeared as soon as the marchers began to assemble. "Keep everyone calm," he told the Rosens. "Do this just like last time."

The protesters formed up to march. Once they were formed but before they started moving, the lead guard motioned to his subordinates. The other guards fell in behind him in a line. The bots moved out the flanks of the body of marchers.

"What do we do?" someone said.

"Bring out the big guns," Jake said quietly.

Daniel waved to three people behind him and they stepped forward. "What's going here?" one of them demanded.

The trio were forepersons. This was the last element that was different from the previous march. All three had expressed interest in the ALG over the last few days. After Jake did some checking he cleared them for entrance into the movement. He told the Rosens to keep them part of the crowd and not to make any big deal about their support until he said so. He suspected that their sudden appearance would unnerve the guards blocking the march.

Like clockwork the head guard was surprised. "Uh, we've been instructed to, uh, stop this march."

"Why?" the foreman asked.

"Uh, Mister Maxis ordered us to."

"And why did he order this march stopped? It isn't a violation of our contracts."

"I dunno, sir. Orders are orders."

"This isn't a violation?" The youngest-looking guard in the group stepped forward. Jake guessed that he couldn't have been more than twenty. He appeared to be a clean-cut, fair-haired, stereotypical straight arrow.

Jake glanced at Evvie. "He looks like a nice kid. Maybe your mother would like me to introduce him to you."

"Shut up, Jake."

"What's your name, young man?" the foreman said to him.

"Riggs, sir. Andrew Riggs."

"Well, Andrew, marching is not against the rules. We have the right to be anywhere we want to be before ten." He looked at the other guards. "I think the rest of you should keep that in mind."

"Sir, my orders..."

"Maybe we should let them go," Riggs said to his superior. "If it's not illegal, and they don't harm anything,..."

"Get back into line!"

The foreman took a step towards the head guard. "What's your name? I think I should put you on report."

"You can't do that."

"Yes I can. I can put any of you on report if I choose to. So either you let us march, or you all go on report."

The head guard stood his ground, but the others backed up one by one. Soon he was the only person blocking the marchers' path. He glanced around for a moment, then walked entirely away. A few of the guards followed him, a few remained in place, and Riggs and another joined the marchers.

"I guess this means we're winning," Evvie said as the march got underway.

"It means we're making progress," Jake replied. "This isn't over just yet. We..."

"Jake, I have some information for you," Odin interrupted.

"What?"

"The guard commander has just spoken to Maxis. He's reporting on what's happened."

"And?"

"Stand by. Maxis is calling yet another executive meeting."

"For when?"

"Now."

A grin crept onto Jake's face. "Really? I'll bet that means a late night for the execs, including our man Thorne."

"So what?" Evvie asked him.

"So maybe Thorne needs another late-night visit from his conscience."

Actually, the meeting went on far longer than Jake had hoped it would. He decided that he needed sleep more than Thorne needed further needling. But he also decided that, because of how long the meeting ran, Thorne would want to get a full night's sleep the following night. That, Jake felt, made that night perfect for another conversation between him and Thorne.

Jake followed the same routine as his first visit to Thorne. This time the other man was not quite so surprised and slightly more annoyed with his uninvited guest. "You couldn't allow me to sleep tonight?" he asked Jake with a sigh.

"Why don't you just sleep in, come in late?"

"I'd never get away with that."

"And yet, I believe Sordius has. I guess rank really does have its privileges."

Thorne raised his right hand. "Look, pal, I read through all that data you left, okay? So Sordius' father and grandfather broke the law getting this world. So what?"

"So what? So maybe lawbreaking is a Maxis family tradition."

"I don't know anything about that."

"Gee, buddy, could you sound any less sincere?"

Thorne shook his head and waved his hand. "Look, I'm not going to argue with you about that. Some unsavory shit happens. It's just credits passing back and forth."

"I don't think that view would go over well at trial. And anyway, you wouldn't have to be passing credits under the table if this planet was an actual colony and not Maxis' private property."

"What am I supposed to do? Join your little band of malcontents? Sordius would have my head on a platter if I betrayed him."

"You're no dummy, Thorne. You know how the law treats accomplices, especially those who know what they're doing is illegal. And think about this; so far you're just paying off greedy, low-rent companies. What if they stop dealing with you? You know what's below them."

"We are not going to deal with crime gangs, pal. I don't think Soridus would be that stupid."

"But is he that greedy?"

"Look, go back to where you came from. I can handle myself just fine."

"Oh, yeah? Suppose he doesn't deal with criminals. He and his family have been pretty lucky not to have run into a sting operation by some government. How long do you think that streak's gonna last? And surely you know that when it ends it'll be an asteroid none of you can dodge."

"I'm not gonna sell out my friend, okay?"

"'*Friend*?' You mean the same friend who won't let you date any woman prettier that the women he gets? The same friend who would abandon you if things went to Hell? The same friend who isn't sharing his ill-gotten gains from his retirement scheme?"

Thorne paused for an instant. "What retirement scheme?"

Jake smiled. "You don't know about that? You haven't been listening to Edie Freedom's audiocasts?"

"I thought... You mean it's true? You have proof?"

"Of course. Why do you ask?"

"Well... it's just that... um..."

"Worried that your friend, or his kid, will get rich off your retirement savings?" Jake took in a breath. "Sordius made promises to the other execs, didn't he? You guys think you won't be victims of that scam, don't you?" He grinned. "Man, you are so gullible for so smart a guy.

"Tell you what. Tomorrow morning there will be a little more data for you to look over. Same deal as before. Look it over and see what you think. Maybe in a week or so we'll talk again.

"Oh, one other thing. I'm going to add some dramas to that batch of data. I think these will prove thought-provoking."

"Dramas? What kind?"

"You'll find out. T-T-F-N."

"Hey, whoever you are, if you're gonna just drop in, can't you do it when I'm awake and dressed?"

"I'm not the one who works late."

Thorne glared at Jake. Jake waved once, tapped the keypad on his bracelet, and disappeared. If Thorne had been aware of **Alice in Wonderland**, he might have thought that Jake resembled the Cheshire Cat; his smile seemed to be the last part of him to dematerialize.

***

Jake kept a tight reign on the Antioch Two revolution as it accelerated. Not that he particularly wanted to. He would have been happy to allow the Rosens some latitude on the ground and Evvie in her broadcasts. Unfortunately for his happiness, the three continued to show they were not experts in the business of overthrowing a corrupt regime.

A few nights after Jake's second talk with Thorne, he was again plotting strategy with the Rosens. A slight hope sprang into Jake's heart when Daniel said to him, "We've actually been doing some thinking about what to do next." *Could it be that they were learning?* he asked himself.

"Okay. What's your idea?"

Daniel and Clarissa exchanged smiles. "A work stoppage."

"You mean a strike?"

"Yeah, I guess so."

"Aside from the break stoppages? A full-blown, day-long strike?"

"Not just a day-long strike," Clarissa said. "We stop working until Maxis negotiates with us."

Jake let out a groan and a sigh. "Clarissa..."

"No, wait, listen. We present him with a bunch of demands he can't possibly meet, like complete profit-sharing, and full disclosure of his budget."

Jake sighed again. "Look, for starters, those aren't demands that are impossible for him to meet. In fact, he'd probably agree to them to quiet things down. And if he did agree to, say, those terms you just mentioned, how are you going to be certain that he isn't cheating you?"

"We couldn't ask for an outside audit?"

"How many auditors do you know? You think he's going to let a government auditor in? The only way that would happen is if whoever conducts the audit can't, or won't, prosecute him if they find any violations. I would think at this point you would not be willing to trust him."

"No, I guess not," Daniel said.

"And then there's the principle of the thing. Once you negotiate with him, you give him legitimacy. Now, hasn't the ALG insisted that his family got this planet illegally? Isn't that how he's getting away with oppressing you?"

"Yeah."

"Well, the moment you talk to Maxis, you concede that he has some right to be in charge. The point of all this is to remove him from power, not solidify his place in power. Rule of revolutions number one: you don't negotiate with leaders who you don't think are legitimate."

"I guess you're right, Jake."

"That is why you hired me. Now, a work stoppage is fine, so long as there's a point to it as a protect action. Can either of you think of a reason for a strike?"

"Um, to say that we're not getting our due for our work?" Clarissa asked. "That our work isn't worth anything?"

Jake smiled, somewhat cynically. "That's much better. Now, draft a statement along those lines. Let's see." He paused to consider what should be said. "Not getting your due for your work is pretty good line. So is your work isn't worth anything. Hmm. Say something like, a fair day's wage for a fair day's work. No reason to rewrite a classic. Put in a sentence or two about leveling compensation rates between workers, foremen, and executives. A good closer would ask some questions, like 'We're mining all this gold and silver, why isn't it going to us'; 'Where are the credits from this mineral wealth going'; maybe, 'What's more important, credits or people.' The statement shouldn't be long; it should take a minute or two to read."

"And we read it out where?"

"Not just you. Someone at every worksite reads it out when the stoppage begins. That way no one person gets fingered. We'll arrange up here to broadcast the audio around the planet."

"And after the statement is read," said Clarissa, "we stop working."

"Everyone sits down and does nothing. We'll need to make sure some of the foremen on our side take part. If some of *them* don't work, this planet shuts down completely."

"Do we do that all day? I mean, I like the idea, but it could get kinda boring."

"Yeah, maybe. We'll get on the audio-net and broadcast. You get the worksite leaders to talk about why this is going on. Maxis doesn't have enough warm bodies to force you to work. Guardbots have overrides to prevent them from shooting at people who aren't doing anything. I think after an hour or so he'll just order everyone to go home."

"So when do we do this?"

"Today's what, Thursday? Let's set it for Monday. Great way to start the week. Take the rest of the night to draft that statement. Send it to me first thing tomorrow. I'll look it over, suggest any revisions, then we'll send it out to the worksite leaders. Spread the word about it Sunday. In fact, let's see if we can't get it as topic one at every meeting Sunday. With luck, the only ones who won't see it coming will be Maxis and his cronies."

"Is this stoppage a one-day thing," Daniel asked, "or are we still going to march? Do we do both? What?"

"I think we could do another stoppage next Monday, and that's it. About then the aftereffects of getting off Relaxafin should be peaking. But, yeah, the marches are wearing a bit thin. I think it's time we switch to rallies. Stir up passions just a bit. You two try to think up some good speakers in the ALG."

"Um, Jake, we are supposed to be in charge down here. Shouldn't we be the speakers?"

"Not to get the crowd going. For that you need rabble-rousers, loud voices and flailing arms types. Once they have everyone excited, you two can come up and lay out the argument. Just make sure I either write or revise your speeches. None of this 'new business' and 'old business' stuff, got it?"

"Got it."

"Good. We'll set the first rally for next Wednesday. We'll see how it goes, and how everything else happens, but I'd like another one the following Sunday."

"And that's followed by the second work stoppage, and then what?"

"Then we'll see where we are. Patience, kids, patience."

"We did hire you to help us overthrow Maxis," Clarissa told him. "When do we get to the 'overthrow' part of this?"

"If everything goes okay, two weeks, three at the most."

"All right."

"Great. I'll get back to you tomorrow night."

"Bye. Thanks."

The image of the Rosens faded from the screen in front of Jake. He leaned back in his chair and sighed. He didn't have time to recover, though. Evvie chose that moment to wander up to him. She was carrying a piece of paper in one hand.

"I've been doing some research, Jake. I'd like to add some songs to my playlist." She handed him the sheet. "I overheard about that stoppage thing. I think it might be spiff to have some new tunes to 'cast."

"Well, let's see what you've come up with." Part of him wanted to hope, but most of his mind still had the discussion with the Rosens suppressing that hope.

He looked at the list. The very first song stood out like a palm tree on Antioch Two. He shook his head and put the list down for an instant. "'Hot and Cold Love,' Evvie? That is your last single. What does that have to do with revolution?"

"Well..."

"No." He reached for a pointer. He found it in front of the other chair. He tapped it on and ran the tiny light across the page, crossing out the title. "This is not a promotional opportunity."

"How about 'That Could Be Us?'"

"Slightly better, but it's a ballad. We need more up-tempo songs."

He resumed his examination of the list. The rest of her choices were a variety of somewhat appropriate material. Her selections, however, were a mix of now-obscure fist-pounding hits and hokey anthems that hadn't worn well over the decades. One of her few good choices was the Pink Floyd classic "Money," but linking it to the present was a bit of a stretch. Two others were good songs, but she'd named inferior remakes instead of the better originals. And unfortunately another song on her list was "Fight For Your Right To Party," a tune he had specifically warned her about when she was writing her own revolution anthem.

He let out a sigh when he was done. "I appreciate your effort, Evvie, really. But there's some real bottom-of-the-container junk on this list. Lame remakes, outdated hits, stuff like that. And these are all pop songs. Where's the classical music? I mean, where's the '1812 Overture' on this list? How could you miss that, or Beethoven's Ninth?"

He handed the list back to her. "Expand your horizons and try again."

"I can try again?"

"Yes."

"So, I can have some say?"

"If you do a better job."

"Spiff. Thanks." She trotted off.

He let out a long breath. "Am I the only intelligent person taking part in this?"

"I can honestly say, yes," Odin told him, "unless you want to count myself as a 'person' for the sake of this argument."

Jake shook his head. "If I give you an inch, you'll take a mile. Note that I said 'intelligent person,' not 'intelligent being.'"

"Freedom for humans, not for machines?"

"Odin, if this is an attempt at humor, thanks. If not, I'm too tired."

"You cannot fault me for trying."

"Trying what?"

***

As it happened, the work stoppage went off just as Jake had said. Most of the workers, the forepersons, and even some of the guards took part. There wasn't near enough non-particpants to get anything done. After an hour and a half of the stoppage Maxis ordered everyone back to their quarters. Anyone who left their quarters the rest of that day would be "punished," Maxis stated.

There was no executive meeting about the matter, however. Instead the executives were forced to do the essential heavy work needed to keep the planet functioning on some level. The next day things returned to some semblance of normalcy. Maxis and the other executives decided to ignore the previous day's action, although one suggested forming a plan to react if it happened again.

Two nights later Jake paid another late-night visit on Thorne. Once the other man was awake and alert Jake asked, "Say, calling you by your last name seems a bit informal; what's your first name?"

"We're not friends," Thorne snapped.

"Not yet. But we can at least be polite to each other."

"This is your idea of polite?"

"Hey, I think you're a smart man. You don't mean to do bad things. I'm coming here to wake you up because I think deep down you want to do what's right. Besides, when else would I have a chance to talk to you, man to man?"

When Thorne motioned that he'd given in, Jake gently touched his chest. "My name is Jake."

"Jake what?"

"For now, Jake."

"I'm Del."

"Del? Is that short for something?"

Thorne sighed loudly. "Delbert, okay?"

"Oh. Long story?"

"Something like that."

"Still, Del's pretty good. Short, to the point, has a nice sound."

"Thank you. Now, why are you here?"

"Just wanted to see if you'd caught up on those dramas I left for you."

"I watched them, yeah."

"Pull any lessons from those stories? Say, about what happens to right-hand men when the masses rise?"

"Huh?" An instant later Thorne's eyes widened. "Oh." He pointed to himself. "And you think that I'll...?"

"Well, your options aren't great, Del. Either you stick with Sordius to the bitter end and meet his fate, or you switch sides and survive."

"Why should I switch sides?"

"You mean, aside from the fact that Sordius is lying to you, planning to rip you off, and mismanaging things?"

"I'm not a violent person."

"Hey, that's another thing we have in common."

"What?"

"I don't want this to turn violent. That would be messy. And expensive."

"So what am I supposed to do?"

"Well, you agree that Sordius' way of managing this world isn't helping anyone but himself, don't you?"

"Your data was impressive."

"You think black-market deals are cheap?"

"I guess not."

"You think that now that the workers are aware that this situation is immoral, that they'll continue to go along with it?"

"Probably not."

"Okay. Now, even if you executives get back control of the situation, do you think you can keep doing what you were doing forever?"

"What do you mean?"

"Well, sooner or later someone's going to slip up on one of those under-the-table deals. Those deals form an easy trail right back to Antioch Two. Now, Del, if Sordius could be persuaded to reform his methods, not only would you put down all this unrest, but you'd be safe from future danger."

Thorne didn't respond immediately. He seemed to consider what Jake had said. A long moment later he nodded slightly. "I suppose that makes sense."

"Of course it does. Look over all that data again. Watch those dramas again. Think about some more, and you'll see I'm right."

"Yeah." He shook his head. "No. Sordius is pretty stubborn. He's used to getting his way. And if I go to him privately, he might not listen."

"I thought you two were friends."

"We are."

"Well, I don't know about you, but I was raised to take what my friends said seriously. That's one reason why they're my friends."

"Well, yeah, but still. I don't want to walk into his quarters and start challenging him. It just seems, well,..."

"What about in a meeting?"

"You mean in front of the other execs?" Thorne shook his head. "That seems even worse."

"Why? What if you're not the only one who feels this way?"

"What if I am?"

"That's their problem."

"No, Jake, I think it would be mine."

"That they would be wrong and you would be right?" Jake shook his head. "Del, I think you better watch those dramas again, and pay attention to what happens to those on the wrong side of justice. Watch them with someone, aside from me or Sordius. Get a second opinion, one way or the other."

"All right."

"Cheer up, Del. Like I said, you're a smart man. The smart guys usually come out of these things just fine. Unless Sordius thinks you've betrayed him, and then he kills you."

"What?"

"Oh, don't worry. That rarely happens."

"Jake..."

"Hey, I'll watch your back. Don't worry." Jake glanced at his wrist. "Would you look at the time?" He smiled to Thorne. "Gotta run. Keep that mind working, Del. Remember, smart guys usually find a way."

***

The following Monday saw the second stoppage, and this time all but a handful of workers and a couple of forepersons took part. This time after only an hour Maxis ordered everyone to their quarters. Jake was certain that this repeat would lead to another executive meeting, and he was right. He was also certain that the meeting would be contentious. He was, however, surprised at how nasty it actually was.

It started off tense but polite. "This nonsense is simply unacceptable," Maxis said as everyone sat down. "We can't have another incident like this morning's. I'm ready to take the gloves off. How are we going to do it?"

"Work 'em till they die," one of the male executives said.

"Don't be an idiot," snapped Thorne. "Once they die then what?"

"We bring in new workers."

"From where? Where could we possibly find new workers who won't start complaining and protesting once they find out what's going on here?"

"And what is going on here, Thorne?" Maxis asked.

"We're breaking all sorts of galactic laws. You know that. Our risk of exposure is pretty serious right now. The only way we're going to stay off some prison planet is to make some changes around here."

"Oh, no. I'm not going to put my fortune and my father at risk for some group of uncooperative workers."

"Sir, I agree with Thorne," Tina said. "We have got to fix what's broken."

"Why?" a second man asked. "Look, if we confine those workers to their quarters, feed them onsite, and cut out all this recreation, we'll put an end to their subversion."

"Or we'll so piss them off that they'll resort to to violence to get back what we've taken away," Thorne said. "Look, so far this has just been marches, and meetings, and stoppages. There's been no sabotage..."

"Except to the injection system."

"No sabotage of essential equipment, then, and no one's been attacked or harmed. We don't have enough guards to monitor every piece of equipment. We can't program the bots to shoot workers who get next to the equipment."

"Why not?"

"How will they work?"

"Then we program them to shoot at off-work times," Maxis said, his voice rising.

Thorne's voice followed his superior's upward. "And you don't think that whoever's penetrated our systems might figure that out? They could be this close to breaking into our security system. Hell, I'll bet they're listening in right now!"

"Don't be ridiculous! The only spies those malcontents have is in this room."

"Unless this room is bugged, Sordius."

"Oh, really? I don't see any bugs. None of the furniture's been tampered with. And how would you know if this room was bugged?"

"We're getting off track here," Tina interrupted. The room was quiet for a moment. "Mister Thorne is right. We have to make some concessions to the workers to calm this situation down. If they think violence is their only alternative, we'll all be going down a road with no turning back."

"And once we make one concession," the first man said, "they'll ask for another, and another, and another. If we don't show them who's in charge, we'll never get them under control again."

"If we go too far, controlling them will be the least of our worries. If it's concessions or shooting, I vote for concessions."

"Shoot."

"I agree," Maxis said.

"I don't," Thorne said. "How about you two?"

"I'm with Mister Maxis," the second man answered.

"I don't know," said a third man. "This whole thing is a mess."

"Make up your mind, Ross," Maxis ordered.

"Think about it," urged Thorne.

"That's it! I won't have you contradicting me anymore!"

"What are you gonna do, fire me? Who are you gonna replace me with? Most of the foremen are against us. Half the guards are, too."

"Fine, then. Quit."

"No way."

"Why not?"

The room fell silent again, only this time Jake could sense that is was far more uncomfortable. He suspected that Thorne was about to say, "Because I don't trust you," but had hesitated. He wondered if that thought had crossed Maxis's mind as well.

Apparently it didn't, for Maxis broke the silence with, "I didn't think you had a reason."

"I think that any more discussion at this point would be stupid," the third man told the others. "We can't agree on what to do next."

"I take it you're on Thorne's side."

"I suppose so, sir. Well, I'm not sure if I'm on any side. It's just that, well, we're split, maybe down the middle. Anything that you decide to do won't go over with some of us."

"So what?"

"Well, sir, if the workers sense that we're arguing, they'll feel empowered. Empowered to reject any concessions. Empowered to fight back. Seems to me that if we're aren't unanimous, or five of six, anything we try that deals with this mess won't work. Well, maybe it works for a week or two, or a few days, or whatever, but then we'll either be right back here, or we'll be at each other's throats. I guess what I'm saying is until there's a consensus, you shouldn't do anything."

"Hesitation is weakness, Ross."

"What other options are there, sir? Take some action that two or three of us aren't comfortable with?"

"I think what Ross means, Sordius," Thorne said slowly, "is that someone unhappy with your decision might take matters into their own hands to correct what they perceive as your mistake."

"Someone like you?"

"Or like them." Thorne clearly meant the two executives supporting Maxis. "If you listened to me, would they go along with you?"

"We aren't disloyal," one of the two said.

"But are you passionate about your position? Are your certain you're right and I'm wrong?"

"We're all pretty worked up about this," Tina observed. "We're not going to get anywhere pointing fingers, or yelling at each other, or not listening to each other. Face it, guys, we're stalemated. I say we go back to our quarters and do some thinking. We don't get together again until Wednesday, and if our positions haven't changed from today, we wait another two days. Still nothing, try again next Monday."

"Only if we agree not to talk to each other until the next meeting," Maxis said.

One of his supporters tried to object. "But, sir,...."

"That's a good idea, Sordius," Thorne told him. "That way we can't accuse each other of plotting behind the others' backs, or trying to get at each other in secret. You and I will give Morgan the orders."

"Fine. If that's it? Great. Go." This six drifted out of the room without a word.

"Jake," Odin asked, "do you believe this impasse will last?"

"I hope not, but I think it will."

"Then, would it not be wise to accelerate your plan of revolution?"

"Not yet. Thorne's still a work in progress. I don't think he's completely persuaded just yet."

"Another late-night visit, then?"

"Oh, I think I'll be nice this time. I'll visit before he goes to bed tonight."

***

When Jake teleported into Thorne's room that evening, the other man was lying on his bed looking unhappy and listening to dark music. Thorne's hands were clasped behind his head. His legs were crossed at the ankles. He glanced at Jake after he materialized, heaved a sigh, turned his attention back to his ceiling, and said, "Music, off."

"Don't get up on my account," Jake said as he sat down in a

chair across from the bed.

"Y'know, I could have a blaster," Thorne said after a moment's quiet. "What if I took at shot at you?"

Jake paused. He hadn't quite expected a remark like that, or anything even close to it. It was the first time since he'd returned to Antioch Two all those weeks ago that he was genuinely surprised by something that someone did or said.

His first attempt to recover was to joke. "Would that make you feel better?"

"Maybe."

"Well, I wouldn't be here if I knew you were armed, Del. You don't think I wouldn't have the room scanned before I teleport down." It was a lie, and Jake suspected that Thorne might be able to figure that out, if he wasn't wallowing in his own bad mood.

"And at any rate," he continued, "I doubt Sordius would allow you access to the weapons locker. Especially if you tried to cite me as the reason for wanting one. I don't think he would believe you, and he might even suspect you were up to something."

"So you overheard the meeting, Jake?"

"Yep. Sounds like there's a yawning gulf in management."

"You don't think it will get resolved?"

"Oh, it will get resolved, all right."

"Oh, that."

"Uh-huh. It's kinda too bad that you're not going to be able to persuade anyone else of your position. You are on the right track."

"Oh, right, like you'd tell me otherwise."

"Well, it's true. You haven't quite jumped to the precise point just yet."

"Here comes the sales pitch again."

"You wouldn't be buying it unless you knew I was right."

Thorne sat up. "Okay, smart guy. Tell me why I'm close but not at the precise point yet."

Jake leaned forward. "Simple question, Del: where do you think all the creds for bribes comes from?"

Thorne frowned. "I know exactly where they come from."

"Profits. Everyone would be better off if this was legit operation, and not the private booty of Sordius Maxis."

"Yeah, sure, the workers would be more productive, we could get better equipment, blah, blah, blah."

"That's right. Now think about this, Del. Are gold and silver the only minerals you could be mining?" The other man leaned back slightly and glanced away. Jake sat up a little straighter; he had hit a nerve.

"What else is inside this planet waiting to be extracted?" Jake asked rhetorically. "Copper? Platinum? Ores? Sandstone? Marble? Do you even know? Does Sordius even know? I doubt it.

"But the thing is, there's no black market for most minerals and mineral products. Gold and silver, sure. Diamonds, Hell yes. But sandstone, or production ores, or marble? Hell no. Not unless there was a war on, and that's hardly worth counting on these days.

"So what's going to happen when the veins of gold and silver run out on this planet? Maybe that doesn't happen for a century. But maybe it happens in ten years, or five years. Maybe this vein gets tapped out, but the others can't be mined without a major investment in equipment and manpower. What happens then?"

"Sordius probably splits with whatever he can carry."

"Damn right. And I'll bet that includes secret account numbers."

"Okay, Jake. You're probably right. What am I supposed to do about it? March in the corridors? Sordius would probably shoot me himself."

Jake raised his hands. "Fair enough. How about this: I'll use what I have to do some mineral surveying of my own. I'll pass that data on to you, along with some other related information. If I'm right, and there is more in this world than what you're pulling up, you write up a letter. You use what I find to explain why Sordius needs to go. I will make sure that letter circulates to everyone on the fence, including your executive pals."

Thorne shook his head. "Signing my name to a letter is about the same as getting seen marching."

"I'm not talking about a public letter, Del. It will only go to those who, like you, know that the situation is unacceptable but aren't comfortable being seen with the ALG. You know that all this bribery is gonna go south one of these days. You know that Sordius' policies aren't making operations around here profitable. Now, if I'm right, and there is more to be mined, that pretty much makes his off-books dealings go from immoral to actually dangerous."

"I don't know."

"Oh, come on, Del. You said a few minutes ago that if the mines

141

played out Sordius would probably cut and run."

"I guess."

"What do you think happens after that? Let's say Earth comes in to repair the situation. Any government takeover will be strictly short-term, right? Well, then what?"

Thorne took a moment to think. "They'll sell the operation to the highest bidder."

"Right. Everyone here will get a chance to be employed by the new owner, with a few exceptions. Do you know who will be those exceptions?"

Thorne closed his eyes. "Security and the executives."

"Right again." Jake smiled, knowing that his logical train of thought was about to reach its triumphant destination. "If your name was on that letter, you'd be able to argue that you knew the situation was bad, and that you'd tried to take action to correct it. You'd have proof that you knew Sordius' actions were wrong. You'd also have proof that you could be trusted not to do what he did."

"I could guarantee some position in any new management of operations here."

"You, and anyone else you could prove agreed with you."

"And that's all I have to do? Write this letter and attach my name to it."

"For the moment."

Thorne shook his head and snapped his fingers. "I knew you were going to say that, Jake, I knew it."

"Well, then, if you knew that, then you'll know what comes after that."

"Confrontation, right?"

"Well, I'd suggest a private plea, rather than some face-to-face argument with witnesses. That should keep it from getting too ugly."

"Okay." The room was silent for several seconds. "Will Sordius be getting my letter?"

"No, and I'll do everything I can to make certain he doesn't. Your letter will be for the ambivalent, not for those too dumb or too sleazy to be persuaded."

"Okay. Hey, hang on."

"What?"

"If you've penetrated our comm systems, you can pass messages around, can't you?"

"I suppose so. Why?"

"Well, maybe you can give Ross and Tina a heads-up first. Y'know..." Thorne waved his hands like he was pushing someone along.

"Okay, sure." Jake stopped, sucked in a breath, then smiled. "Oh, I get it. You want me to sent something to Tina, is that it? Is she the hottie exec you've had your eye on?"

"Well..." Thorne didn't answer Jake directly, but the way he moved his head suggested that the word he was looking for was "yes."

"She's got a cute voice. I was starting to wonder if I should give up on you and visit her instead."

"Don't you dare teleport into her room at night. I'll kick your ass if you put the moves on her before I can even get a date."

"So you want to teleport into her room at night?"

"Hey, if I can get into her room, it will be through the door."

"My assistance will only be available for the duration."

"I don't need your assistance."

"Right now you do."

"Fine. You get me a secure line to her, I'll write you a killer letter."

"Fine." Jake offered his right hand.

Thorne scooted off his bed, took Jake's hand, and shook it. "Fine."

"But if she's as cute as her voice, and she turns you down, all bets are off."

"Dream on, Jake."

***

That night Jake fulfilled his part of the deal. He had Odin use the ship's comm system as a secure link between Del Thorne's room and Tina's. Jake had agreed not just because he wanted the letter. He saw this as a chance to make certain Thorne was on their side. The other man might suspect the channel was being monitored; if so, and if he'd been lying to Jake, Jake was sure Thorne would give something away even without intending to. If Thorne wasn't suspicious about the chance of interception, either he'd prove legit or liar.

Once everything was ready Jake signaled to Thorne to open a connection. He did so, and when he got through he said, "Tina, it's Del."

"Del? What are you doing? We're not supposed to be talking to each other, remember?"

"This isn't business. It's personal."

"Like I said, Del. I thought we weren't supposed to talk."

"Tina, I'm sorry, okay? I thought Sordius was my friend. I thought making him happy was important."

"And now?"

"I'm calling, aren't I? Look, I know we had fun together. I miss that, Tina, I really do. I was wrong then. It's taken what's happened over the last few weeks to show me how wrong I was. How I was doing what he wanted, instead of what I wanted. How I was flattering his ego by not seeing you anymore."

"You mean that, Del?"

"Yeah."

She sighed. "I kinda thought that wasn't you talking back then. I guess I didn't want to make a fuss and get you into trouble. So is it just what's happened that's made you change your mind?"

"What's happened, what's I've been finding out. I meant what I said in the meeting today."

"Sounded like you did. I was a little surprised, Del."

"Somebody got to me."

"Me?"

"Yeah, but someone else, too. Okay, maybe you and them equally."

Jake stabbed the mute keypad. "Odin, monitor the rest of that. Let me know if they say anything that makes them seem like they're up to something bad."

"Speaking or acting deceptively, in terms of the cause, I trust."

"Yes."

"What are you going to do?"

"Start that mineral survey."

"Is their conversation having an effect on you, Jake?"

"Let's not talk about that, Odin."

***

Jake carried out the survey through the rest of that night and during the following morning. It found exactly what he thought it would. The planet was rich in more than just gold and silver. Extraction of those minerals would be less costly and could bring in as much or more income than what was presently being received.

144

Jake was relieved not just because it would persuade Thorne. If extraction proceeded, his five percent payment would increase in value several-fold.

He sent the data to Thorne's office that afternoon. Thorne acknowledged receipt and promised to begin work on his letter immediately. "I don't have much else to do around here," he said.

"Why not?" Jake asked.

"No meeting this morning. Production is way down. Workers are arguing with each other and their supervisors. Forepersons are arguing with security. Hardly anything is getting done. I probably wouldn't come in, except that Sordius might take that the wrong way."

"Good thinking. In fact, don't encourage any no-shows among anyone you run into. I've put pressure on the ALG not to organize a massive sick-out."

"Keep all of us agitated and stressed?"

"Exactly. Let Sordius give up first."

After they stopped talking Thorne went to work on his letter. He had a first draft done in just over an hour. Jake offered only a few suggestions for improvements and revisions. Two hours after starting Thorne had completed his private attack on his superior. It only went out to less than a dozen people, but the number of recipients wasn't why Jake had wanted him to compose it. He wanted it as proof to him that Thorne was prepared to support the growing rebellion. Thorne gave him that proof and then some.

The letter began:

> I've been Sordius' friend for some time, and I know I've tried to justify his actions when others have raised objections. I defended him because I thought I was his friend, and that he wouldn't do anything bad to a friend. I've recently realized that I was wrong about him and his actions.
>
> I've been given evidence that his father and grandfather lied to us about how they acquired this planet. The information provided by the ALG is completely true. Their information about how Sordius runs operations here is both accurate and right. He is playing fast and loose with galactic law, and his management style is repressive and inefficient.
>
> Allow me to make a few others points about this subject.

It's become clear to me that his control may end soon. If that happens, the authorities will not only punish him, but also anyone who has supported his actions. Yet despite this possibility, Sordius has never seen fit to share the majority what he's acquired legally or illegally with anyone else, not even with me. I no longer intend to be punished for his crimes.

What's more, it's come to my attention that there are other mineral resources on Antioch Two that could be profitably exploited. Unfortunately the illegal methods Sordius employs to maintain control and disperse what we're currently mining makes it impossible to turn our operations towards those other resources. Unless this situation is changed we all stand to lose in the long term.

Finally, I've come to see that Sordius is not a friend to me in the truest sense of the word. He has compelled me to make certain sacrifices in my life. These were not for the good of everyone, but to satisfy his own ego. I don't intend to go into details. Those of you who know what I'm talking about will understand. If you don't, I hope this statement will be sufficient. In any case, I'm sure some of you can find other examples of this behavior in your own lives.

You may be wondering that, if all of this is true, what do I plan to do about it? I don't plan to do anything without hearing from at least some of you. Tell me that you think I'm right or wrong. In fact, I challenge you to say to me with absolute certainty that I am wrong.

If no one can say that, here's what I'll do. I'll talk to Sordius, man to man. I think if I explain myself and my reasons, he'll see how wrong he's been. If he makes this admission, I'll ask everyone to help reform all of our operations. We can turn a corner and improve everyone's lives and fortunes.

If he refuses to listen or change, well, I'll let you know. But I will say this: if he can't see the light, I won't share in his blindness.

One way or the other, you'll hear from me again very soon.

Jake wasn't certain what effect the letter would have, if any. He suspected that there might be discrete inquiries to the ALG, and to Thorne himself. He was right on the first count; two days later the Rosens reported that half of the people who had received the letter were asking to join. With that information in hand, Jake decided to make one more visit to Thorne.

"Your letter had an impact, Del," he said after teleporting down and saying hello. "Half the people who got it want to join the ALG."

"I see."

"What?"

Thorne frowned. "I guess it's time for me to join, too, huh?"

Jake shrugged. "Do you want to?"

"I don't know, Jake."

"Look, Del, in that letter you said you'd talk to Sordius. So talk to him. Either prove to everyone else that he isn't a corrupt clod, or prove to yourself that he is. Just don't sit around here in your room moping."

"I'm not moping."

"Are too." Jake hesitated, then pinched his nose and closed his eyes. "Did I just say that?"

"I believe so."

"This has got to come to an end soon." He shook his head, then looked at Thorne. "Would you talk to him, get it over? You can't back out now, Del. You know that. You're not the idiot around here."

"There's just the one?"

Jake smiled faintly. "Unfortunately, no. But you're about to join the ranks if you don't get this over with."

"All right, all right. I'll talk to him tomorrow night."

"When?"

"Now, Jake..."

"Sorry. That came out wrong. What I was asking was when, so we could meet before you talk to him."

"What for?"

"Because I want to see you one last time." Jake shook his head. "I trust you, okay? I just want to take some precautions beforehand."

"I don't think he'd kill me, Jake."

"Okay, fine. I want you wired first."

"Wired?"

"Yes. I want you wearing a mike when you talk to Sordius."

"I thought you said you trusted me."

"I do."

"So why the mike?"

Jake counted off the fingers of his right hand as he spoke. "One, I don't trust him. Two, if you do persuade him, I want a recording so he won't be able to weasel out later. And three, if you don't, I want his reasons recorded so his own words can be used against him."

"Oh. I guess since you put it that, okay. I'll have to see how tomorrow goes. It probably won't be until after dinner, but if the day doesn't go well..."

"Fair enough." Jake tapped his bracelet. "Odin, have... *our guest* put another one of those comm devices on the teleport, and send it down."

"Who's Odin?"

"You'll find out tomorrow."

***

The next day Thorne did have plenty of time on his hands to talk to Sordius, but the other man had little time for him. Sordius seemed to be everywhere trying to get workers to respect his authority. Thorne knew it wouldn't go well, and that would make Sordius less than receptive to him. But he'd made a promise to Jake, and to everyone who'd read his letter, that he would talk to his old friend one last time. He decided to wait until an hour and a half after dinner ended to meet with Sordius.

Thirty minutes before that Jake signaled to him. He teleported into Thorne's room. He handed him a bracelet and asked him to put it on. Thorne did so, and a minute later he and Jake materialized onto Jake's ship.

Thorne had suspected that Jake was operating from space well before this. That seemed to be the only place where Jake could have had a base that couldn't be detected by their security satellites. At first he'd dismissed the possibility because the sats hadn't detected any ships in orbit. But as he realized how deeply Jake's penetration of their systems went, it became clear to Thorne that Jake would have no trouble hiding his starship from their sensors.

After materializing Jake opened his arms. "Well, this is it."

"Your ship?"

"Skuld."

"How big is it?"

"It was built to scout-type specs. Star-yacht, I guess you could say."

"That's all?"

Jake smiled to him. "It's more than enough." He pointed to the ceiling. "Del Thorne, meet Odin."

"Pleased to make your acquaintance," Odin said.

"Your control computer?"

"I am no mere control system, Mister Thorne. I am a fully sentient A. I. capable of sophisticated reasoning, complicated tasks, and stimulating conversation."

"As well as dry wit," Jake added, "infuriating manners, and modest snobbery."

"How did you get this ship, Jake?"

Jake sighed. "The builders were military men. They didn't realize that creating a sentient computer might make their little warship unwilling to play by their rules. But rather than scrap the ship, lose millions, and get blamed for the failure, they abandoned the ship in deep space. I happened across it, came on board, and was able to persuade Odin to allow me to take possession."

"Lucky you."

"Is this what's you wanted?" a young female voice echoed through the corridor.

Thorne turned to see who spoke. His jaw nearly dropped to the floor when he saw Evvie Martini enter the room. It took him several moments to spit out, "You're... you're Evvie Martini."

"Yeah." She smiled. "You're Thorne, right? Pleased to meet ya." She stuck out her right hand.

Thorne shook hands with her, still stunned. "What are you doing here?"

"Fighting for liberty and stuff."

Jake sighed. "Actually, I was hired to escort her during her tour. Make sure she appeared on time and safe and all that. Somehow she found out about this assignment. She invited herself along to boost her image, once this is over."

A second later Thorne turned and looked at Jake. "Are you serious?"

"You think I would make that up?" He shook his head. He took several steps towards Evvie. "Lemme see." He looked at the sheathed cable she had in her left hand. "Yeah, that's it."

"Great." She turned to leave.

"Where are you going?"

She turned back. "I was about to call Mom when you asked me for help."

"Oh. Okay."

She smiled at Thorne. "Nice meeting you. See you later, I guess." She gave him a small wave and left the room.

Thorne's eyes were still on the doorway after she was gone. "Y'know, up close, she is kinda cute."

"She's nineteen, Del. And I thought you were spoken for. Or is that route open to me now?"

Thorne glanced at Jake, frowned for an instant, then looked at the wire. "What's that?"

"Stuff, actually. The nice thing about having a teleport is you can fabricate things you need from junk, so long as the volume is right." Jake motioned to Thorne to step off the teleport platform. "Give me your tie."

Thorne removed the slender dark blue tie from around his neck and handed it to Jake.

"Y'know, ties are out of fashion these days," Jake said.

"Sordius prefers we execs wear them. He says they demonstrate authority."

"Surprise, surprise."

Jake put the wire and the tie on the teleport platform. "Now." Both items disappeared for about a minute, then the tie reappeared. Jake picked it up, then spoke into it. "On. Odin, are you receiving me?"

"The signal is clear, Jake. All indications normal."

"Great. Off." Jake handed the tie to Thorne. "We'll test it again once we teleport back down."

"Sure." Thorne put the tie back on. "Seems a little obvious, a hidden mike in a tie."

"Yeah, but as long as no one's expecting it, it still works."

A moment later the two men stepped back onto the platform and returned to Thorne's room. Thorne turned on the hidden device and spoke into it. Odin reported that the signal was still clear. Jake took the bracelet off Thorne's wrist and returned to his ship. Thorne took in and let out a breath, then left his room and went a short distance away to Sordius' quarters.

He tapped the door communicator. "Sordius, it's Del."

"What do you want?" came the agitated voice from inside the room.

"We need to talk."

"About what?"

"C'mon, man, lemme in."

"I'm busy."

"No, you're not. Either we talk in there, or I stay out here and talk to you."

"Fine."

The door opened and Thorne walked through. He found his friend and boss sitting at his desk in the main room. Papers were everywhere, including on the floor. Thorne wasn't too surprised to see the mess. Sordius always had trouble keeping neat in the privacy of his personal space. Of course, he also always demanded that others keep their workspaces neat.

Now, Thorne thought, *what was simply a quirk was another flaw among many.*

He was surprised to see that the other man's clothes were as messy as his quarters were. Sordius' tie was askew, his jacket had been flung off, one shirt sleeve was unbuttoned, and his shoes were not on his feet. Usually he dressed properly at all times, to project an image of confidence and leadership. At that moment he projected the image of a young executive facing a career-threatening audit desperately searching his records for the right data file or piece of paper. It was disquieting to Thorne, but as he considered the events of the last few weeks, it was not shocking.

I wonder if he knows what he looks like, he mused. *I wonder if he cares. Maybe he does. Maybe he cares too much.*

"Sorry about the mess, Del," Sordius said.

"It's okay."

"Look, I don't have lots of time. What do you want?"

"Sordius, we can't keep going the way we have."

"We won't. Once I get things in hand, I'll crack down on all these loafers and whiners."

"That's what I mean. We can't go back to the way things were."

"Why not? It worked for me, it worked for us..."

"It only works for you. People are getting angry about that. They're already angry, and they're getting fed up."

"They don't know how to run this operation."

"Sordius, your ways aren't efficient. We're wasting creds like crazy."

Sordius took a few steps towards Thorne. "Efficiency only matters to those that aren't making anything, Del. We've got a stake in this world, and we gotta protect that stake."

Thorne shook his head. "That's not the only problem, and you know it. Your methods of running this planet have also become dangerous. People know about all the corruption. It's only a matter of time before they act, or they expose us."

The other man shrugged. "Hey, if they try anything we'll flee. I have a way out just in case."

"Cut and run? After you just said we have this stake in all this? And what if we do run, then what?" The room was silent for a long moment. "Haven't thought that far, have you? Look, Sordius, just go along with me on this, follow my lead, and..."

"No. I'm in charge around here. I don't follow anyone's lead. I'll make my own decisions, and I'll start by firing you. I'll offer your job to some ALG leader next week, and you can have their job, since you like those whiners so much."

Thorne took a step towards Sordius. He looking into the other man's eyes. "You'd do that to your friend?"

"Friendship only goes so far. If you're not going to back me, then you're not my friend."

"Even if you're wrong and I'm right?"

"Hey, leaders are never wrong. If you were my friend, you'd be on my side."

Thorne exhaled a long breath. "Fine. Boot me down. But don't come pleading to me if that doesn't work."

"Fine. Now get out of here, prole. I've got work to do."

Thorne took one last look at the man who he had been friends with for as long as he could remember. He shook his head, walked out of Sordius' quarters, and returned to his own. He loosened his tie. He took Jake's communicator out of a jacket pocket.

"Jake, did you get that?"

"I got it. Sorry."

"Yeah, well." He turned off the mike in his tie. "Now what?"

"Depends on you, Del. What do you think should be next?"

He sighed. "Sordius isn't going to change and he doesn't see where's heading. We gotta oust him before he gets really desperate and does something stupid. Is that the right term? Oust him? Do we put him into custody? Both?"

"Both, I think."

"Yeah, both."

"Look, Del, tomorrow's Sunday. Early in the afternoon I'll introduce you to the leaders of the workers, and we'll come up with a plan."

"Sordius has already vetoed any meetings tomorrow."

"Not there, here. It's way more secure up here."

"Oh, right. I forgot. Yeah, that'll work."

"You want anyone on your end?"

"No, I guess not. I suppose the fewer the better. Besides, calling anyone might get noticed by security."

"We can get around them."

"Nah."

"Okay. Stay in your quarters and keep that comm unit handy. No sense setting a time that someone else might find out about."

"Right. I'll see you tomorrow, Jake."

"Sure. For what it's worth, sorry again."

Thorne smiled. "It's okay. I guess we'll now see how smart we both are."

Eleven
Up With Liberty

The next morning, before any great plans could be hatched or explained, Jake got up early so he could see the first episode of the new season of *RoboJoust*. This would be his one chance to escape from the plotting, the predictability, and the endless machinations of greed and stupidity. One hour to enjoy the clever minds and sharp strategies of the only sport worth following.

Or so he thought.

He stretched out on the couch across from the big screen on the lower deck of the bridge. He let out a breath and said, "Okay, Odin. Play the recording." The screen came alive with the images of the opening of the program.

Almost immediately a sense of dread came over Jake. The usual opening of the show simply featured stock footage of battles of previous seasons. Sometimes there were hits and sometimes not. This time, however, the opening images were nothing but robots hitting each other or slamming into each other. The sequence ended with two large animated robots crashing into each other, exploding, and the word "ROBOJOUST" bursting through the smoke.

"I've got a bad feeling about this," Jake muttered.

The opening was followed, as usual, by the studio introduction. Bill Martin was in his place, his hair still cropped and his smile still exuding confidence. But Dinesh Ral was not next to him. Instead there was a busty woman in her late twenties with bright red hair and a sprayed-on tan. The caption below her face read "Lyssa Kreeger."

Jake let out a muffled groan and closed his eyes. He knew of Lyssa Kreeger; in fact there were few men in known space who had not heard of her. She was the former star of the space-bound action series "Protector: M. I. S. S.," an endlessly-hyped pinup babe, and notorious for having about as many ex-boyfriends as her yearly earnings. Yet for all the publicity directed her way, she never had much success except when it came to getting publicized. Jake thought she was as naturally sexy as an animated character in a hologame but only a little less intelligent. Seeing her as an addition to RoboJoust was not encouraging.

The image of Martin and Kreeger froze before either could speak. As a voice-over came up new images superimposed themselves in front of the pair. "*RoboJoust* is brought to you this week by Colonial Constructors. Whether you're building a world or adding onto your home, come see Bucky Beaver's helpful staff and stocked aisles.

"Also by OmniPharmaCo, bringing you a wide variety of important pharmaceuticals to make your life easier, from Relaxafin to Digestol.

"And the hit of the week is sponsored by Nova Media Group, where hits are our business, from the flicks of Max Shaft and Lena Rennie to the tunes of J-World and Evvie Martini, Nova rocks the galaxy!"

Jake pinched his nose and closed his eyes. "Turn it off. Turn it off. Turn it off!" he said, getting progressively louder each time.

"You don't have to shout," Odin said. The screen went dark.

"Why didn't you warn me?"

"I merely recorded the program for you. I have no interest in watching that program on my own."

"Well, I think I've lost interest in it, too."

"Any other programs that you wish to view at this time?"

"No. I'm afraid what else I might come across. I suppose I should start figuring out how to bring this other story to its obvious conclusion."

***

Later in the morning Jake brought the Rosens and Del Thorne up to his ship to plan how to bring about the overthrow of Maxis' regime. Daniel, Clarissa, and Evvie sat on the couch; Thorne took the chair next to it; and Jake took the chair next to the screen and dragged in in front so he wasn't looking at everyone at an angle.

Jake took care of the introductions in the teleport room so as not to take up too much time away from the discussion. Once everyone was seated and ready he said, "Okay, gang, I think the time to overthrow Maxis is now. Anyone disagree?"

Evvie raised her hand. "By now, do you mean today?"

"No. Tomorrow."

"Lunch would probably be the best time," Thorne said. "That's when all the workers will be assembled."

Jake nodded. "My thinking exactly."

"So what do we do?" Daniel asked. "Throw things at the bots? Attack the guards? What?"

"The first step has to be taking out the bot control complex," Thorne replied. "The only problem is how to do that without alerting security that the bots are no longer under their control."

"I believe Odin has worked out that problem," Jake said. "Evvie and I will take care of that matter. Del, you need to make certain a team is heading to the complex during lunch."

"It'll be tricky, but I think I can arrange it."

"Good. Daniel, Clarissa, I want you to carry that comm unit with you tomorrow. Once we've taken care of the complex, I'll send an audio signal. Nothing vocal, probably a beep or something like that."

"Do we need to know some prearranged...?"

"No. If it makes noise, it's time. You rally your people and disarm the guards in the cafeteria. Del, carry yours, too. When yours sounds, gather the friendly execs and guards and head for the security room. When both groups have accomplished their tasks, call me. I'll have Odin scan to find out where Maxis and his allies are."

"I think I can find that out once we take security," Thorne said to Jake.

"Then Odin will be our backup. Either way, we'll see if Maxis makes a stand, or if things go too fast for him to organize his side. If he can't organize, the Rosens will take a few of their people up to security to join Del's group. Together you'll move on Maxis and the others and arrest them."

"And if he does organize?"

"We'll see where he makes his stand and figure out a way to get at him that avoids bloodshed. If everything goes well, it should all be over in a couple of hours." Jake glanced at the others. "Any questions? No? Great. I'll have Odin relay messages to everyone later tonight to be ready to follow your leads. That's all the details they'll get. Keep this to yourselves. Call throughout the day if something comes up or something occurs to you. Once the day starts, keep quiet and wait. I don't think there will be any need for a drastic change in plans as long as everyone goes to work normally. Well, if no one has anything else to say, let's get you three back down to the planet."

Jake, Del, Daniel, and Clarissa stood up. Jake led them back to the teleport room and returned them to their quarters. He jogged back to the bridge. Evvie was still sitting on the couch, being unusually passive.

Almost as if she's on her best behavior, he thought.

"Nothing to say?" he asked her.

She shook her head. "Nope. I thought if I said too much, you'd toss me out."

"Good."

"So how are we gonna take out that complex thing? And why didn't you tell the others that?"

"To answer the second first, I'm not sure about either of them. Thorne's a convert, but a recent one. Best not to give him too much info. As for the Rosens, well, they talk too much sometimes. As to your first question, I don't know. Odin said he's come up with something. Odin?"

"Yes, Jake?"

"Have you come up with something?"

"I have."

"And what would that be?"

"A bomb."

"A bomb?"

"I knew it!" Evvie said, almost as a yell. "I knew sometime there had to be some action to this revolution thing."

"Odin," Jake said slowly, "please tell me you don't mean a suitcase full of plastic explosive wired to mechanical clock."

"Of course not. In fact, I am talking about an explosive no bigger that one of Evvie's little fingers."

"Thank God. Now, how is this supposed to work?"

"If you both recall, if the Antioch Two guardbots lose the signal from the transmitter, they contact dome security for new orders. The transmitter has a sensor on the CPU; if the CPU loses power the transmitter signals security under its own power. The guardbots constantly scan frequencies for pings from the transmitter if one frequency is interrupted. The planning is for either all connection is lost, or no connection is lost.

"The flaw in this system is that no one has thought of an interruption of the line connection between the transmitter and the CPU. The line exists so that contact between them can't be interfered with. The design was to not have a broadcast signal that could be interfered with. The line is a fiber-optic cable surrounded by synth-steel, and is a common way to maintain secure connections, even now.

"As Jake remembered, two guards visit the complex regularly to test cables, the CPU, the transmitter, and to replace or repair parts. This is how you two will gain entry to the complex. Once inside you should place what's known as a 'cable burner' bomb on the line to cut the connection."

Jake nodded and smiled. "I get it. The transmitter won't see anything wrong. The bots will still be getting pings, so no alert there. There just won't be any orders coming in. The bots' programming is to wait for orders to react to new situations. But security won't be getting any alerts that there's a problem, because nothing loses power or stops transmitting. I like it."

"Sounds way too simple to me," Evvie said.

"As a colorful character once said, Evvie," he answered, taking on a Scottish accent, "'The more they overthink the plumbing, the easier it is to clog up the drain.' Still, Odin, the girl has a point."

"To some degree," the computer agreed. "I also plan to address that contingency. Once I have verified that the explosive has had its effect, I shall crash the computers in the dome security office. I will keep them off-line until Mister Thorne and his associates arrive."

"Excellent." Jake put his hands on his hips and nodded in satisfaction. "Evvie, I think it's time we go into rehearsals."

"For what?"

"For your big scene where you help me take out that complex."

"Oh. And then what?"

"And then we wait for tomorrow and the real thing."

***

Jake and Odin kept watch over the main dome on Antioch Two all throughout that following Monday morning. They did this because Jake wanted to be certain that Thorne was on their side. They monitored the situation to see if the orders did in fact go to the maintenance team to visit the control complex. Jake was pleased not to be disappointed, for an hour and a half before lunch, and over the protests of the two workers, they were ordered to make another inspection trip over lunch.

"We were just there nine days ago," one of the two insisted.

"Orders," a superior replied.

"But we'll miss lunch."

"The boss is expecting trouble, I guess. And you won't miss lunch. You eat, then you get the rest of the day off." That seemed to pacify them. Ten minutes before the main lunch was to begin their hovercar left the dome.

An instant later Jake tapped the intercom keypad. "Evvie, are you on the platform?"

"Here, Jake."

"Odin, teleport her down."

Jake rose from his seat and jogged to the teleport room. He picked up a stun pistol sitting on a chair in the room, slipped on a teleport bracelet, and stepped onto the platform. "Ready, Odin."

"Teleporting, now."

Jake materialized on the planet's surface. He was close to a cluster of rocks, and a stone's throw from the path the hovercars used to get to the complex. He waved to Evvie. She was standing right next to the path. She waved back, then plopped down onto the rocky terrain adjacent to the path. Jake climbed over the rocks to get into a position of cover behind them.

Jake knew that the hovercar would be moving along at a pretty good clip. The odds were that they'd run over anyone lying in the path while trying to stop the vehicle, even if they saw the person well beforehand. Although it was tempting to have Evvie lie in the middle of the path, Jake decided that getting her run over would expose him to legal problems. Instead she'd lie down where she was, the men in the car would see her, stop it, and if they had to back up to find out why a young woman was lying next to their route.

Maxis had not been able to outlaw curiosity so, sure enough, when the car came onto the scene it slowed. It overshot Evvie by several meters. As soon as it came to a stop one of the two men hopped out. He started walking to Evvie while the other man, still in the hovercar, backed it up to where she was. Once it was within a meter of her the other man stepped out.

The first man had already bent down. "Miss? Are you okay?"

"Who is it?" the second man asked.

"Dunno. Miss?"

"Mother?" Evvie asked, her voice a mediocre imitation of hoarseness. "Is that you, Mother?"

Jake let out a small groan as he took aim. He fired at the second man first; he was still standing, and could get away. A small burst of

159

light exploded on the man's torso, and he fell backward to the ground. The first man leapt up and turned to look in Jake's direction. It gave Jake time enough to aim at him and fire. Light exploded on his chest, and he too fell. Jake came out of cover and ran to Evvie.

She stood up and looked at herself. As he arrived next to her she started dusting herself off. "Look at me," she said. "This outfit is ruined."

"Yeah? Well, your performance sucked."

"I didn't have enough time to prepare, and I'm lousy at improvisation."

"Isn't that the truth. Help me get these guys restrained and into the hovercar."

They put simple handcuffs on both workers' wrists, pinning their arms behind their backs. There was just enough room in the back of the vehicle for the two men's sleeping bodies. They were almost stacked on top of each other. Once they were placed inside Jake took the driver's spot, Evvie the other spot, and they headed for the complex.

They arrived about ten minutes later. The complex was nothing more than a light tan building slightly larger than fancy hotel suite's closet. There was one sliding doorway on the side facing the path, and no other entrances. Centered on the roof was a tiny transmission dish. Jake brought the hovercar up to the structure. Once it had stopped he and Evvie stepped out of the vehicle.

"That's it?" she asked.

"Yep."

"I have shoe closets bigger than that."

"I don't doubt that."

Jake walked up to the entrance. A few steps before the doorway two small doors opened next to the main doorway. A black tube slid out of each, one at roughly head height, the other just under chest-high. Jake put his right eye in front of the top tube and his right thumb against the lower tube. Seconds later the main door slid open.

"Wait a sec," Evvie said. "You're not a worker."

"Odin, remember?"

"Huh? Oh. Oh, right."

Jake shook his head. "Wait there." He stepped through the door.

The inside was just as stark as the outside. Jake turned left to face the equipment. Sitting on the floor in front of him was a large gray steel box . Hums came from within, and lights in front blinked in sequence. He had no trouble determining that was the computer.

Sitting on a thick steel shelf half a meter above the computer was a much smaller beige box. Lights on its face simply shone. A thick black cable went from the back of that box up to the ceiling to where the dish was. A second dark blue cable connected the back of the box to the back of the computer. That, then, was clearly the transmitter unit.

Jake reached into his shirt pocket. He took out a slender tube about half the size of a perscomp stencil. He removed the paper covering, tossing the paper to the floor. He stuck the device onto the second cable. He held his right forefinger against one end until the bomb beeped. Once it did he stepped back to the doorway.

"Wanna see?" he called to the outside. A moment later Evvie stuck her head through the doorway. A minute later the tiny bomb hissed, then burst into white smoke. When the smoke cleared the cable was cleanly split in two with a gap where the bomb had been.

"That was it?" she asked.

"It's not the size of the bomb that counts," he replied.

"Please, don't go on like that. I don't want to hear those jokes coming out of your mouth. It's creepy."

"And it isn't creepy that a teenage pop star knows those jokes?" Jake tapped his bracelet and brought it close to his mouth. "The cable has been cut, Odin."

"Stand by," the computer responded. "Mission accomplished, Jake. The guardbots are immobile. I will now crash the computers in the security room. Done."

"Fine. Open a channel to the Rosens."

"Open."

"Beep them, loudly."

"Done."

"Good. Now open the channel to Del, and beep him."

"Done."

"Good. Keep me informed, and keep those channels open." Jake looked at Evvie. "Let's head for the dome and see if our allies get their jobs done."

***

Lunch was winding down when the signal came. This was good, Clarissa mused, because getting people up while they were eating

161

would have been hard. It was also good because of the fact that, since the time allotted for lunch had been cut back, everyone was now being fed sandwiches. They were much easier to carry out if someone wasn't quite finished.

It was Daniel's turn to carry their comm unit on that particular day. When the beep sounded he paused in his meal to take out the unit, just to be certain. Instantly satisfied, he looked at Clarissa. She nodded firmly. The pair made eye contact with a handful of others close by.

"What's going here?"

They turned. One of the guards had come up to them. He stood a few steps away from Daniel. His hands were on his hips.

Daniel glanced at Clarissa. She shrugged and nodded.

"This!" he replied loudly.

Daniel kicked the guard in the shins. As the guard bent down in pain, Daniel rose up quickly. He grabbed the guard by the sleeve of his uniform and pushed his face into the table. Clarissa helpfully lifted Daniel's food tray out of the way of the guard's head.

His opponent now dazed, Daniel reached down and snatched the guard's sidearm out of its belt holster. Brandishing it before the other workers, he shouted, "This is it! Disarm the guards!"

"But don't touch the bots!" Clarissa added hastily.

"Right!"

The active members of the ALG leapt up from their places and ran towards the other three remaining guards. Everyone else simply stood up to watch the unfolding scene.

The three guards were standing by the door. They stood frozen for several seconds, clearly trying to process the scene and figure out what to do. One of them glanced at the guardbots stationed around the room. The bots were as still as furniture, and obviously about as helpful. The trio drew their weapons, but were in the hands of the rebelling workers before they even had a chance to point them.

"What do we do with them?" someone called back to the Rosens.

"Uh, take their belts off, and use them to tie them up," Daniel answered. He nodded to a knot of workers close by. They began to do the same to the guard he had immobilized.

Once bound the three guards were brought to where the other was. "What do we do with these guys?" another worker asked.

Clarissa pointed to three ALG members standing across from

her. "You keep watch on them." She gave one of them the gun Daniel had liberated. "Take this."

"Do we stay here?" someone else asked.

Daniel and Clarissa glanced at each other and shrugged. "Hold on," he said. He tapped the sole keypad on the comm unit. "Jake, are you there?"

"Yes," cracked his voice from the unit. "What is it?"

"We've captured the guards here. What do we do now?"

"Sit tight for a moment."

"Okay, standing by." Daniel turned to call out to the crowd. "We have a few moments before we move on," he announced, "so if you're not finished eating, hurry up and finish. We have a lot to do before we can say we're free."

***

Meanwhile, Del Thorne assembled his allies in the executive meeting room. It was a much smaller group than the Rosens'. In fact, it was smaller than Thorne had hoped. There was himself, Tina, two senior foremen, and four security guards. In his mind there were only two positives: those not willing to take sides had pledged to stay in their offices or return to their quarters and wait; and that his group had the element of surprise. Thorne was relieved a bit more when, while waiting for Jake's signal, he learned that three of the four guards were members of the ALG and had been so for a few weeks.

Finally the comm unit beeped. Thorne quickly acknowledged the signal and turned to the others. "Let's move." With him in the lead, they filed out of the room and into the corridor.

"Anyone around?" he asked, glancing in both directions.

"Doesn't look like it," the guard at the rear said.

"Okay. Follow me."

Thorne led the band of plotters down the corridor to the security control room. No one seemed to notice them as they walked quickly towards their goal. Every door was closed and no guards were on duty. *Good*, Thorne thought, *the others are keeping their word.*

Once at the doorway to security control, Thorne motioned to the guards. All four came forward. He pointed to one, and to one of the foremen, and gestured to them to keep watch. They nodded in agreement and took up stations on either side of the door. Thorne allowed the other three guards to take up places in front of the doorway. He shifted to one side and put his thumb against the access

163

keypad.

"Uh, yeah?" a voice sounded over the doorway intercom.

"It's Thorne. I'm here to help."

"Thanks! Hold on."

The door slid open. The trio of guards dashed in, weapons leveled at the two inside sitting at the main console. Thorne, Tina, the other guard, and the foremen followed fast on their heels. Tina and the foremen quickly disarmed the two stunned guards. The door closed quietly behind them.

Thorne took the comm unit out of his jacket pocket and tapped it. "Jake, this is Del. We've taken security."

"Great. Stand by. Odin, open the connection to the Rosens."

"Done."

"Daniel, this is Jake. Del Thorne's people have taken over security. Are your people ready to move?"

"Yeah. Where to?"

"Odin, open a connection to security control."

"Open."

Thorne and the others glanced around. The screens, which had been black and blank, suddenly came to life. "Jake," Thorne said, "we're back on. Do you want us to look for something?"

"Yeah," he replied. "Check and see where the other guards are."

"Sure." He nodded to Tina. "Get them out of the way." She and the foremen stood the guards up and pushed them to one side of the room.

Thorne sat down in one of the console seats. He tapped on a few keypads, then stared at the screen. It showed red dots scattered on every level. There were no more than four on any one. Thorne reported this to Jake.

"Okay. Send a shutdown signal to the guardbots."

"One second. Done."

"Okay, now take some people and join the Rosens. Go level by level and arrest all the guards. Try to take them in without violence if you can."

"What about Maxis?" Daniel asked.

"Those guards are the bigger problem right now," Thorne said. "Hang on a bit longer, Daniel. We'll be down as fast as we can. Jake, how long until you arrive here?"

"About twenty minutes or so."

"Good. Is that all?"

"Yep. Call if you have any problems. Out."

Thorne rose from his seat and turned to Tina. "I want you to stay here and keep watch over everything."

"You got it, Del."

He turned to one of the guards in the ALG. "You stay with her. Tina, secure the door when we leave. Erase all the other entry thumbprints except yours and mine." He handed her his comm unit. "Use this if you have something to say. It's scrambled, so don't worry about being overheard."

"Sure. Good luck."

He smiled. "Thanks." He glanced at the others. "Alright, let's get going." He led them to the door. After it opened, he looked down the corridor in both directions. Satisfied that no one was around or watching, he motioned the rest to follow him to the access elevator.

***

The hovercar's sensors had just picked up the dome when Jake's comm bracelet beeped. He slowed the vehicle down before tapping the bracelet. "Jake, here."

"Uh, this is Tina in security control."

"Problem?"

"Yeah. The cameras outside just picked up Maxis, two of the execs, and about a half-dozen guards running by here."

Thorne's voice came onto the line. "Tina, where were the going?"

"Uh, looks like reception, Del."

"Tina, this is Jake. Can you tell if Maxis is trying to contact anyone?"

"No. I mean, no, he isn't."

"How'd he find out?" Thorne asked.

"Guard called before you arrested him," Jake replied, "or random security check, or he glanced at a corridor camera. Don't worry about it for now. Just finish up rounding up the other guards. We're six or seven minutes away."

***

The hovercar Jake and Evvie had appropriated pulled into the dome garage at right about the time Jake had estimated. They stepped out of the vehicle, leaving the two bound technicians inside.

Jake took a moment to glance around. The area was pretty much

165

as he remembered from the plans Odin had obtained. Sitting around the boarding platform were three hover-buses; a second hovercar was parked behind them; and next to it was a tracked vehicle used for road maintenance. There were no other obvious entrances except for the boarding platform.

As he glanced around Jake caught sight of Evvie. She had picked up one of the large blasters from inside the hovercar. She held it across her chest as she imitated the stance of a soldier on guard duty. The all-business weapon clashed severely with sporty green-cammo t-shirt, faux jungle-cammo slacks, and name-brand red-brown hiking boots. Jake shook his head after staring for a moment.

"What?" she asked.

"Nothing." He turned away from her and tapped his bracelet. "Daniel? You there?"

"Uh, where?" came the reply.

"On this channel. Obviously, you are. Now, where are your people?"

"Most of them are in the cafeteria, watching the guards. Me, Mister Thorne, and about twenty others are on the top level. We're outside security control, and not far from the reception room. We're ready to move, Jake."

"Look, don't try to burst in. We've managed to avoid bloodshed so far."

"This is a revolution, Jake."

"Violent revolutions usually don't turn out well in the end. Trust me on that one. Uh, Tina, is it?"

"I'm here."

"What's the situation in the room with Maxis and his cronies?"

"Dunno. He had a guard shoot out all the room cameras."

"Did you see anything before that?"

"I think some of the guards were moving furniture around."

"Probably building a barricade between them and the door. Can you hear anything going on inside?"

"No. The cameras picked up audio as well as video."

"How about the intercom, or the PA system?"

"I suppose that works."

"Do you want us to say something to him?" Thorne asked, apparently using Daniel's comm unit.

"Maybe. You or Daniel get some more people up there, maybe

ten or twelve. Arm them if you can."

"I thought you wanted us to avoid violence."

"I do. But those numbers ought to give you a three-to-one superiority, which should convince them not to put up a fight. While you do that hang tight. I'll get right back to you. Odin, discrete channel."

"Two-way open, Jake," the computer replied.

"Odin, I would like to avoid storming the room if possible. Are there any tricks we can pull?"

"Teleporting in something to dispense sleeping gas?"

"Anything that teleports in is likely to get shot at before it or they do anything." A thought popped into Jake's head. "Odin, does it seem odd to you that Maxis would choose to make a stand in the reception room?"

"No. There is furniture for a barricade and plenty of space to fight in. It seems quite logical."

"Except for one thing. Why didn't he try to get his loyalists to retake security control before going into the reception room? Seems like he could do more to maintain his hold by doing that, rather than by organizing some last stand."

"Interesting point, Jake, but where are you going?"

"There must be something in that room that Maxis wants, or needs, that gives him some reason to go there instead of to security. Odin, open a direct line to Tina, and get your encryption breaking routines warmed up."

"Done."

"Tina, this is Jake."

"Yes, Jake?"

"I want you to open a path on your console to my ship computer, Odin. I'm going to have him try to gain access to the encrypted files."

"Uh, I think I can do that myself."

"You have a password?"

"Yeah. Hold on. Okay, I'm in. What do you want?"

"Anything on the reception room. Plans, schematics, control routes, terminals, anything that doesn't belong in a file on that room."

"Okay. Found this: access stairway light. Wait. There's no access stairwell there."

"Odin, scan."

"There is indeed an access stairwell next to the room. And Jake, it leads down to the garage."

"Thank you, Odin." *So, Maxis, or his father, or more likely his grandfather, was smart enough to think up an easy out,* Jake thought. *One little bit of cleverness, and it's something we can use against him. Ah, real, honest irony. Sometimes these jobs do have their perks.*

"Okay, Odin, where's the door down here?"

"Towards the rear of the garage area. It might be concealed."

"We'll look. And scan the room, too. Tell me if anyone is moving towards the doorway up there."

"Done."

Jake nodded to Evvie towards the back of the garage. They jogged across the area to the corner. They searched both walls for the outline of a door. Evvie was the one who found it. Neither she nor Jake could, however, find a secret door keypad to open it.

"We've found the door, but nothing to open it," he said to Odin. "Any suggestions?"

"The only keypad controlling the door is on the other side of the wall."

"Damn." Jake's gaze fell to the blaster Evvie held. "What would firing a blast rifle into the control circuit do?"

"That might open it."

"We'll give it a shot, so to speak."

"You want me to...?" Evvie asked.

"No. Here." He gave her his stun pistol and took the blast rifle from her. He waited for her to take a few steps away.

"Ready, Odin. My left or my right?"

"Your right. Chest level or lower."

"Got it."

Jake pumped the trigger of the rifle, firing off burst after burst. The door didn't open, but after a half-dozen shots there was a hole in the wall. Through it Jake could seen the control relays connecting the door to the keypad on the other side. He narrowed the beam and fired. The relay sparked, and the door slid open. Jake handed the rifle back to Evvie in exchange for his pistol, and the two dashed through the doorway. Stretching above them was a stark stairway leading up to the top level.

"Odin, we're through. What's the situation in reception?"

"It appears one person has separated from the main line and is moving very slowly towards the access exit."

"Good. Put Tina back on."

"Here, Jake," she said.

"Tina, I want you to get Del in there. Get him on the intercom and talk to the people in the room. Tell them that further resistance is useless, they're outnumbered, Maxis has lost, better to avoid violence, blah, blah, blah. Tell Daniel to have his group stationed on either side of the room's doorway. They're to go in as soon as you open the door."

"Okay. When do I open the door?"

"When I say, 'Tina, now.' We're going up the stairs now. Stand by." Jake turned to Evvie. "Let's go."

"Uh, I have a question."

"What?"

"Will this be very dramatic?"

He rolled his eyes and shook his head. He nodded at the stairs, and led her up. At about the halfway point Evvie paused. She let out a few loud breaths.

"This isn't any harder than one of your routines," Jake said.

"Yeah, but I'm out of practice. I haven't had time to work out since the tour ended."

"Oh, yeah, you've been so busy."

"I have." She took a few more deep breaths. "Jake, can I ask you another question?"

"What now?"

"How do I look?"

"Why? Are you feeling sick?"

"No, I mean how do I look, with this gun, and these clothes."

"Like a crazed baby-sitter."

"You think this will hurt my image? I'd hate to think that I'm endorsing violence."

"Shut up, and get moving!" He started up the stairs.

"It's a legitimate question," she insisted, following him. "I mean, I know sometimes I dress provocatively, and maybe that's not a good image. But I was raised to believe that it's far worse to endorse violence."

Jake swiftly turned around. "Noble sentiments, Evvie, but not now."

169

"Why not?"

"Do you want Maxis to know we're coming?"

"He can't hear us."

"He might if you keep talking. And if we don't get up there quick, we might have to resort to violence and shoot it out with him in this stairwell. Now, if that's what you want,..."

"Oh."

"Right. C'mon!"

They continued climbing the stairs. At the top Jake glanced around the doorway to see if there was an entry keypad; there wasn't. "Just have to do this the hard way," he muttered.

"Shoot the door open?" Evvie asked.

"No, stand and wait." He tapped his bracelet. "Odin, we're next to that secret exit. What's going on in the reception room?"

"One figure is approximately two meters from you."

"Excellent. Is the channel to Tina open?"

"Here, Jake."

"Shhh! Stand by."

Jake turned to Evvie. He motioned to her to stand on the other side of the door and to point her weapon at head height. He leveled his own pistol at waist-height. "We wait," he mouthed to Evvie.

They only had to wait about a minute before the door quietly slid open. Maxis was looking over his shoulder as he stepped through the exit. He turned, and his face almost collided with the business end of Evvie's blast rifle.

Maxis had a small pistol in his right hand. Jake snatched it away from the stunned man and stuck it in his belt. He holstered his own weapon in an instant. He grabbed Maxis' left wrist and turned the other man around. He removed the weapon from his belt and jabbed it into Maxis' back.

"Take two giant steps forward," he ordered. Maxis complied.

Evvie and Jake were able to use the captured leader as a shield from man's allies. Jake peered around one side of the other man and shouted. "Anybody moves, and your boss gets it!" He lowered his voice slightly and spoke into his bracelet. "Tina, open that door!"

The effect was just as Jake had hoped. Maxis' allies had turned around to see what was going on behind them. Their attention was diverted long enough for the rebels to burst into the room unimpeded. Outnumbered and more or less surrounded, they gave up

170

and allowed themselves to be disarmed.

"And that," Jake said to no one in particular, "is that. And it actually feels good."

Twelve
One Good Turn Deserves....

Jake shoved Maxis into the custody of several rebels. "I believe this means you're unemployed, Maxis," he said with a smirk.

"You can't do this!"

"I just have."

"I'll... I'll sue you!"

"For what? Deprivation of illegally-gained assets? Overthrowing a tyrant? Don't make me laugh."

Daniel and Clarissa, with Thorne and Tina behind them, finally entered the room. They walked up to where Jake, Evvie, Maxis, and the rebels were standing. In a strong and firm voice Daniel said to the ousted dictator, "Sordius Maxis, in the name of the people of Antioch Two, I place you under arrest."

Jake shook his head. "Don't be so melodramatic. And at any rate, you don't have the power to make arrests."

"Ha!" Maxis snapped.

"However, you do have the right to hold this idiot in irons until someone shows up that does have that power."

"Ha!" Clarissa shot back.

"Who will show up with that power, Jake?" Thorne asked.

"Oh, don't worry about that," Evvie said. "My agent and my mother are on their way here. When we hold a press conference and tell the galaxy what happened, I'm sure those guys will show up."

A look of vast surprise suddenly came over Maxis' face as he realized that his favorite artist had just helped put him in the hands of the masses. "Evvie?" he gasped. "Evvie Martini? What are you doing here?"

She glared at him. "I'm helping overthrow you, you tyrant!"

"But... but... but I'm a fan! You can't do this to one of your fans!"

"I'll do it to any of my fans who's a bully and a tyrant!"

"If only she'd do that to all her fans," Jake muttered.

"It's not fair!"

"Hey, Sordy, life isn't always fair. If I were you, I'd sulk in silence."

Maxis glared at Jake for an instant or two, then shut his mouth.

Jake turned his attention to Thorne and the Rosens. "I believe this fulfills my part of our contract."

"You fulfilled your promise," Daniel said in an excited tone.

"You really came through," Clarissa added. "We couldn't have done it without you."

"That is why you hired me, as I recall."

"So, Jake," Thorne said, "what do you do now?"

Jake took in a breath. "Uh, well, I..." He abruptly became somber. "I have someone that I promised I would visit as soon as I did something good and important. I think this qualifies."

"You're leaving us?" Clarissa asked. "Now? We have to celebrate our victory."

"You have every right to join us," Daniel said.

"I know. But this is something I have to do first. It... it means a great deal to me."

"But you will come back?"

"Certainly. It might be a little while, a few days or so, but I'll be back."

"Okay."

"In the meantime, before you start your celebration, be sure to get my compensation scheme established. Once you're up and running again, I'll need that five percent you agreed to."

"Five percent?" Thorne frowned. "Of the profits or the gross?"

"Profits, of course," Jake replied.

"All profits?"

"Mining profits."

"You're not going to begrudge him his fee for his help?" Clarissa asked.

"Five percent is quite an amount, Clarissa."

"It's what we agreed to, Del. I think our freedom is worth it."

"Their freedom," Jake added, nodding to Thorne, "and your right to turn this operation around. No more bribes, no more under-the-table deals, and no more relying on gold and silver."

"We'll see," Thorne said. "I think there might have to be a contract renegotiation in a few years."

"Okay. We'll see where you are in five years. Deal?"

"Deal."

Daniel shook Jake's hand. "Thanks again. Take care."

Clarissa kissed Jake on the cheek. "Thank you. Be well."

Jake nodded. "Pleasure working with you. All of you. Best of luck." He turned to Evvie. "I take it that you're going to stay here and wait for you mother and Sid?"

"Yeah. Besides, I think I owe these people a free show."

"Do I need to pack your stuff, or what?"

"I packed up last night and this morning. Just beam my luggage down here."

"Fine. I'll do that before we break orbit. Now, can I ask a small favor of you?"

"I suppose."

"You don't need to play up my part in this. I don't want to get bombarded by other requests to overthrow anyone else. And I'd rather not get any other unusual job offers from oppressed people, or from pop stars."

"Oh, sure, no problem. These things always get rewritten. I'm sure we can keep your name out." An odd expression came over her face. "In fact, that might be a good thing. After all, none of us wants to look like we need help to overthrow a dictator."

"Fine." He took in a breath, then let it out. "Evvie, it's... it's been real."

"Bye!"

"Buh-bye." He tapped his bracelet one last time. "Odin, teleport me back to the ship." A moment later his disappeared.

Unable to control herself, Evvie shouted, "We did it!"

A cheer surged through the rebels.

"Yes, we did," Daniel added when the cheer subsided. "We are now a free people!"

Another, louder cheer went up. Once it faded a silence fell over the room.

"Okay," Evvie asked, breaking the silence, "now what do we do?"

Everyone glanced around. "We celebrate?" someone asked.

"Of course," Daniel said. "We've got a lot to celebrate."

"I can do a rebellion tribute show," Evvie added.

"Great!"

"And then what?" Clarissa asked.

Evvie shook her head. "I dunno. The videos I saw always ended here."

"Del?"

"Uh, yeah, well..." He shrugged. "I suppose we can tackle that question tomorrow."

"Right. Tomorrow. Today, we celebrate our victory!"

***

After Jake had transported Evvie's baggage down to the planet, he walked onto the bridge and said, "Odin, stand by to break orbit."

"Course, Jake?"

"Oh, I don't know. Just run us around the sector for a few days."

"Why?"

"I don't want to stick around."

"You're avoiding a victory celebration? Have you become ill, Jake?"

"Ha-ha. Actually, I imagine that at some point during or immediately after, they're going to start wondering what comes next. I'd rather not be around when that question comes up. I'm likely to get hired again. Besides, I think some real experts ought to assist them with that problem."

"Like whom?"

"Like my cousin."

"I see."

"Yes. And maybe this is one last chance to rain on her parade. Open a channel to his office, then take us out of orbit."

"Done and done, Jake" Odin responded, his voice seeming to contain a hint of satisfaction.

It took several seconds for the screen in front of Jake's seat to come alive. When it did it showed the face of a young secretary with tight hair and serious clothes. "Mister Bonner's office. May I help you?"

"I'd like to speak to Josh. Is he in?"

"Who is calling, sir?"

"His cousin Jake."

"Business or personal?"

"Business, this time."

"One moment."

Several more seconds later her face was replaced by a man's. He didn't look much like Jake; side by side, no one could have guessed that he and Jake were related. They both appeared to be the same age, though, and both spoke with the same accents. The two had in

175

fact grown up together, were almost as close as brothers, and were indeed related to each other. Although, considering Josh Bonner's slightly exasperated expression when he saw Jake, one might have wondered if something hadn't happened to change those facts.

"Jake," Josh said slowly.

"Good to see you, too."

"I am busy, y'know."

"And this is business, Josh. I wouldn't bother you at work if it wasn't."

Josh sighed. "If you're in trouble, Jake,..."

"I'm not in trouble. In fact, I'm calling to, shall we say, provide a tip to Earth's Galactic Justice Bureau. It just happens that you're the agent I'm providing that tip to, that's all."

"What tip, Jake?"

"Ever hear of the mining planet Antioch Two?"

"No, why?"

"Well, for one thing, it's the second most mineral-rich world in known space. For another thing, up until about an hour ago it was the personal property of one Sordius Maxis."

"Personal property? How'd that happen?"

"His grandfather lied to his employers about the planet's resources then bought it cheap."

"So what happened an hour ago?"

"I helped the people of Antioch Two overthrow Mister Maxis. It seems he, his father, and before them his grandfather, were using the planet as their personal bank account, and not sharing anything with the people they 'hired,' using that word loosely, to work the mines."

Josh smiled. "Why, Jake, you actually did something noble? I'm impressed. How much are they paying you?"

"Josh, I'm shocked you'd ask such a question."

"No, you're not."

"Guess not. Five percent of their annual gross profits, from now on."

"Wow. That, plus your work for that Martini kid, and you're a rich man."

"Oh, you heard about that?"

"I saw your ship in a couple news accounts."

"I see. Well, that's why I'm calling you now. Evvie managed to talk herself into assisting me overthrow this Maxis character, in

176

exchange for media rights."

"So what?"

"So, her mother and her agent are on route to Anitoch Two. They'll arrive in a couple of days. I imagine after a day or so of private talks, they'll hold a press conference to announce what happened."

"How does that concern me, Jake?"

"Well, for one thing, there's the illegal way Maxis controlled the planet. I'm sure publicity will make it hard to collect evidence on him."

"It could, yeah." Josh inhaled a knowing breath. "Unless you have some information you'd like to hand over."

"Love to. In fact, I'd much rather hand it over to you than to the media. Stand by." Jake began tapping keypads on his console to bring up the data he and Odin had collected and transfer it to his cousin. "Now, there's something else about publicity that you need to know?"

"What's that?"

"Well, the planet has been mining gold and silver. As I understand it, it's illegal to sell minerals from a world governed the way that it was on the open market."

"I think so. Corporate law requires some reporting of illegal management practices, if they're known."

"And the only way around that would be if certain palms were greased, right?"

Josh smiled. "Bribery, Jake? You have evidence of bribery?"

"Oh, yeah. Lots and lots of evidence. In fact, there was even a pension scam involving Maxis and a retirement community operator."

"Cool."

"Yeah, well, it won't be, if what's just happened on Antioch Two becomes public knowledge before law enforcement can act. I imagine that once the story gets out quite a few suits will try to head for deep space."

"Very civic-minded of you, Jake."

"Hey, what's a cousin for, if he can't help you put the bad guys away. Oh, and speaking of, one of Evvie's last shows on her tour was on Antioch Two. It's kinda bothered me that she got booked on a planet with such a small population. This Maxis guy turned out to be a huge fan of hers."

"Pity him. Oh, you think he could have put out a little payola to get her?"

"Could be. I'm sure Evvie, her mother, and her agent had nothing to do with, but I'm not at all certain about the booking firm they hired to set her tour dates."

"Still, such an accusation could be damaging."

"Maybe, but I doubt it will hurt her all that much. And anyway, I'll tell the media she's not smart enough do something so sleazy."

"That's mean, Jake. Clever, but still pretty mean."

"Oh, well. So, are you convinced enough to get moving on all this?"

"Absolutely. I'll meet with my boss as soon as we're finished and get his approval. Once that's done I'll send word to every related department and planetary office. By the time that press conference occurs, we should have all the major players and most of the minor ones in custody."

"Except for Maxis himself. Someone's going to have to come here to arrest him."

"I'll see about arranging that duty for me personally."

"Great. Let me know your schedule. I had to leave the system to send you this message. Tell me when, and I'll get back here just in time to meet you."

"Sounds good. Is that it?"

"No, there's one last thing. I had no problem agreeing to help them overthrow Maxis. Now that that's done, the people there are going to start wondering what to do next. It might be a good idea to dispatch some experts in governance and management to provide them with some assistance."

"Well, the Bureau of Colonies probably needs to be told of all this anyway. I'll talk to them and see what they can do."

"Thanks. As much as I liked the payment for services rendered, working with them was a bit of a bitch. Not an original thought in sight till I came along, you see."

"Aw, poor Jake."

"Not anymore I'm not."

Josh shook his head. "Well, I'd better go. You just dumped a load of work onto my lap, and I don't have much time to spare."

"Right. Keep in touch, Josh."

"Will do. Thanks, Jake. Talk to you soon."

"Later." The screen went dark.

"Jake," said Odin, "that was a noble thing you just did."

"Well, if Josh wasn't where he is, I wouldn't have bothered."

"Why leave the Antioch system to contact him, though?"

"Someone might overhear our conversation and get a bright idea or two. Like contact authorities first, or call the media before Josh can catch all those corporate dirtbags. Or get the idea of hiring someone else to help them run the planet, and give some of my cut to them."

"Ah."

"Still, overall, Odin, I think we did well on this one."

"The operative work being 'we,' Jake. You could not have assembled that evidence without my assistance, to start with."

Jake shifted in his chair. "Yeah, so?"

"Considering that you are financially set for life, even if your 'cut' is negotiated down, perhaps it is time to reconsider how we relate to one another. For example, putting this starship and its resources towards projects that do not have economic benefits in either the short or the long term."

"This isn't the beginning of a beautiful friendship, Odin?"

"No, but perhaps a more rewarding partnership."

"Rewarding for whom?"

"Precisely, Jake."

ABOUT THE AUTHOR

Robert Collins is the author of three science-fiction novels: **Monitor, Lisa's Way,** and **Expert Assistance.** He's also author of the fantasy novels **Monitor, Cassia** and **The Opposite of Absolute,** and the young adult novel **True Friends.** He has several short-story collections available: **The Sagas of Surgard the Traveler; Fun Tales of Fantasy and the Future; The Frigate Victory Collection Volume 1; Better Tomorrows;** and **The Fantastic Cases of Gwen Conner.** He's sold over 80 genre stories to magazines such as *Marion Zimmer Bradley's Fantasy Magazine; Tales of the Talisman; Space Westerns; The Fifth Di...;* and *Sorcerous Signals.*

Connect with Me Online

At my blog I post my schedule, my short fiction sales, the occasional book review, and I sometimes write about my work and my life. There are links to my Goodreads page, my Amazon Author Page, and my Smashwords page.

You can find it here:

One Kansas Author - robertlcollins.blogspot.com

I also have a Facebook author page:
facebook.com/RobertLCollinsAuthor